LUCKY JIM

MEMOIRS OF A RANDLORD

BY

J B TAYLOR

LUCKY JIM
MEMOIRS OF A RANDLORD

BY

J B TAYLOR

EDITED BY T S EMSLIE

STONEWALL BOOKS

'Standing behind you like a stone wall'

2003

First published by Hutchinson & Co in 1939
under the title *A Pioneer Looks Back*

ISBN 0-620-29508-2

STONEWALL BOOKS

52 MAIN ROAD • ST JAMES • CAPE TOWN • 7945 • SOUTH AFRICA

Distributed in Southern Africa by Book Promotions
P O Box 5 • Plumstead • 7800 • South Africa
Tel: 021-706-0949 • Fax: 021-706-0940
email: orders@bookpro.co.za
and in the United Kingdom by Central Books
99 Wallis Road • London • E9 5LN • England
Tel: 020-8986-4854 • Fax: 020-8533-5821
email: orders@centralbooks.com

COVER DESIGNED BY THE DESIGN HOUSE
SET BY THE DESIGN HOUSE
PRINTED AND BOUND IN THE REPUBLIC OF SOUTH AFRICA
BY CREDA COMMUNICATIONS

The publisher wishes to express thanks to:

Michael Reitz for his interest and assistance,
and especially for Lucky Jim *on False Bay at dawn;*

Nick Taylor for his support and enthusiasm,
and especially for 'Lucky Jim' on the cover;

Eric Woods, whose father Percy was a regular
companion of 'the Grand Old Man of False Bay.'
Thanks, Babe, for the book—and much else besides.

LUCKY JIM AND THE FISHING FLEET ON FALSE BAY AT DAWN, WITH DENEYS REITZ IN THE BOW

'I have fished on False Bay off and on for twenty years, and during the latter half of this time my boys have fished with me, always during the Parliamentary Sessions.

False Bay is aptly named. Unlike Table Bay on the opposite side of the Cape Peninsula, it is a treacherous expanse. Dead calm one moment, and then fierce south-easters beat in from the Antarctic; the waves lash mountain-high, everything on board bangs and pitches from rail to rail, and one has to run for shelter without loss of time.

The mouth of the bay is thirty miles wide and from the Cape of Good Hope to Cape Hangklip it lies open to the great swells rolling in; and it requires good seamanship to navigate its stormy reaches in an open boat.

But the weather is not always rough, and the days I best remember are those when we sailed at dawn, the surface smooth as glass. As the fog slowly lifted, we saw vast flocks of malagasy duck and terns and seagull and cormorant diving into the shoals of sardine, the fall of the birds lashing and churning the sea like shellfire in France.

Amid this hurly-burly come schools of porpoise, a whale or two, and seals and penguins and sharks, the whole forming a spectacle probably unequalled anywhere in the world. Then we throw out our lines and pull in great fish—Cape Salmon, cabillaud, Steenbras and other kinds weighing from fifteen to thirty-five pounds and more—until our fingers are numbed and the boat is down by the head with the weight of our capture.

We used to go out on *Lucky Jim*, an eleven tonner belonging to our friend Mr Jim Taylor, the Grand Old Man of False Bay. He was possessed of great wealth and great kindness. He held broad, tolerant views on South African affairs, and his knowledge of the Bay and its moods was unrivalled. As often as wind and weather permitted, he took us with him, and many are the happy hours we spent in his company.'

Deneys Reitz
No Outspan
1943

Preface

It has been a great pleasure to read and co-ordinate Mr J B Taylor's manuscripts and notes, which he has from time to time written about the events of his long and interesting life. It does not fall to the lot of many men to crowd into their lives so many history-making episodes, especially during a period when South Africa was emerging from lethargy and commencing a career which revolved round the production of gold and diamonds, destined from the date of their discovery to arouse the elements of strife and bloodshed and the passions of strong men.

As Mr Taylor's story relates, he and Mr Hermann Eckstein, in the early days of their partnership, commencing in 1886, had no idea when Mr Alfred Beit established them in Johannesburg that they were destined to become two of the foundation stones of the great Rand gold-mining industry. Each of them at a comparatively early age left South Africa to reside in England. Hermann Eckstein died soon after he had settled in London, whereas Mr Taylor lived to enjoy with his family the life which only the England of those days could offer to one who could afford to live a country life. There he enjoyed the sport of foxhunting, shooting and fishing, till in the evening of his life a new South Africa called him back to the land of his birth.

Mr Taylor's reminiscences record that he was not only blessed with a great capacity for enjoyment and giving enjoyment to his friends, but that he possessed the rare faculty, given to few who have made fortunes in mining camps, of being able to cast the lure of money-making behind, and leave stocks and shares and company promoting to those who have no other hobby.

In compiling these memoirs, I have been criticised for using the word 'Kaffir' to designate the South African aborigine of Bantu origin. Today they are called 'Natives,' or 'the Bantu people,' but in the days of which Mr Taylor writes, all aborigines were called 'Kaffirs,' with, I must admit, no knowledge of the derivation of the word, and certainly no knowledge of its correct spelling. A Boer in those days spoke of 'the Kaffirs' and 'my Kaffirs,' meaning 'my servants.' Therefore I have used throughout the following pages the name by which the black people of Africa were known when the diamond diggings and the goldfields were discovered.

I would like to express my thanks to Mr B Bennion of Johannesburg for his kind assistance in guiding my pen in style and punctuation.

In helping to present these memoirs to the public, I cannot adequately express to Mr Taylor my appreciation of the patience he has shown in furnishing me with replies, which I was obliged to obtain before putting his story into the sequence in which it is compiled.

H O'Kelly Webber
Author of *The Grip of Gold*

Foreword

It has been a great privilege to me to have lived for seventy-eight years, and during most of that time to have been in close touch with one of the most interesting periods of world history; and I cannot adequately express my gratitude for having been permitted to take part in the development of such a wonderful country as South Africa, and for having had the opportunity of enjoying the friendship and respect of such men as Cecil Rhodes, Alfred Beit, Paul Kruger, Louis Botha, and others who laid the foundation of the prosperity which we South Africans enjoy today.

J B Taylor

St James
Cape of Good Hope
1939

Contents

List of Illustrations

Chapter 1

Early Days

I was born in Cape Town in December 1860. For those who know the city today it must be difficult to realise that it was then little more than a calling station for ships going to and from the East.

I used to hear from my father the story of the steamship *Alabama*, whose captain, Semmes by name, was a friend of his. It will be remembered that the *Alabama* belonged to the Confederate Government in the American Civil War. She was a brig-rigged steamer equipped as a commerce raider, and her mission was to destroy all merchant vessels sailing under the flag of the Northern States of America. She was hung round with chains, which acted like armour plating. She had been chasing a sailing-vessel called the *Sea Bride* which tried to escape by coming into Table Bay. This vessel was, however, caught by the *Alabama* before she reached the three-mile limit, and was towed in as a prize. Later on the *Alabama* just escaped destruction by an enemy vessel as she was leaving the Cape waters. After many exciting experiences she was eventually sent to the bottom of the sea off the coast of France by the American warship *Kearsage*. Captain Semmes escaped and was picked up by an English yacht.

We lived in the Gardens above Cape Town in a thatched house called *Heynes House*, built in the Old Dutch style with beautiful moulded gables. There was a *solder*, or small platform, high up, which was accessible only from an outside staircase. From this height we had a lovely view of Cape Town and Table Bay. In the distance we could see the long curve of beach, named many years later Milnerton, after Lord Milner, and the panorama was backed by the Tigerberg Hills and the mountains beyond.

The slopes of Table Mountain and the Lion's Head were covered with silver trees, proteas, heather, and innumerable wild flowers. Many of those flowers are now extinct, the great white anemones have been uprooted, and the proteas have been cut down by the coloured people for fuel.

In my day the roadstead of Table Bay was open, and there was no shelter for vessels from the northwest winds, which often became gales in the winter months. The great gale of 1865 was disastrous, and a number of ships were blown on to the beach opposite the Castle.

At that time my Aunt Ellen was on a visit to us, and one of the first things I can remember is that she took me up the outside staircase on to the little platform to watch the ships being battered and tossed about by the gale.

It is curious how one remembers little things that make a lasting impression on the childish mind, such as the wild spew of the sea mingled with the flying leaves which obscured the view as they were driven by the gale. Even today I can recall how my long curls blew across my eyes and how intrigued I was as I watched my aunt's clever management of her crinoline against the force of the gale. It was not an ideal costume for windy weather. It billowed and bulged and seemed to be possessed of a frantic desire to encompass her neck or blow over her head or anywhere except where fashion and decency intended it to be.

For a long time afterwards we used to find during our walks along the beach the wreckage of ships that had been blown ashore. The steamship *Athens* lay on the rocks for years before the sea broke her up finally; although she had made a great effort to keep her head under steam to the gale, she was eventually blown ashore. All hands perished, including the captain and his wife. It was said that he must have been reading the ship's large Bible when the loss of his vessel became inevitable, because it was found on the beach; it is now in the Cape Town Museum. The ship's boiler is still to be seen on the rocks near Somerset Hospital.

CAPTAIN SEMMES OF THE *ALABAMA*, 1863

At the age of ten I was sent to a school called Dalton School. It was situated in Roeland Street, on the outskirts of the town at the foot of the De Waal Drive. Today this street is connected in one's mind with the city gaol, although at that time it was a fashionable thoroughfare. The school was owned by a man of the name of Oscar Dalton Guallier, and my master's name was Baines, a man cursed with a violent temper. On one occasion he caught me in the act of drawing a caricature of himself on my writing-pad, and he promptly administered a smart box on my ears. I retaliated by flinging an inkpot at him. This so enraged him that he hauled me into an upper classroom and gave me such a sound thrashing that I had to be sent home in a cab and given a vinegar bath to counteract the effects of it. The ink-splash remained on the wall for many years to mark the scene of my ill-timed wit; at least, so I have been told by Mr Herbert and Postmaster-General Lenton, both colleagues of mine today on the Board of the *Overseas Communication of South Africa*. They well remembered the episode.

However, I did not stay long at Dalton's School, for which I had not many regrets.

* * *

In those days the great event of the year was the Queen's birthday celebrations. Everyone collected on the Parade to watch the trooping of the colour; salutes were fired and garrison regiments paraded in full force. It was a gay scene, and besides the European entourage of the Governor and his staff all the principal residents of the town and countryside, including the Malays and hosts of coloured people, crowded together to watch and join in the revels.

The Malays wore picturesque garments, and instead of shoes they wore wooden clogs. This national dress has now, alas, been almost entirely superseded by European clothes. The women's dresses of the gayest colours imaginable had voluminous skirts, beneath which they wore innumerable petticoats of every hue, possibly an attempt at imitation of the crinoline fashion. In place of hats they wore gaily-coloured handkerchiefs, draped in Indian fashion over their heads and shoulders.

SIXTEEN VESSELS WRECKED IN TABLE BAY IN 1865
VIEW TAKEN FROM THE CASTLE GATEWAY

The men's garb was no less picturesque, though somewhat more sombre. They wore long, flowing coats, in some cases embroidered with silver and gold and bright colours, and on their heads turbans, fezzes, or enormous plaited-straw hats like umbrellas. The priests were distinguished by their white robes and white and gold turbans.

A great feature of the entertainment was the hawking of confectionery and sweetmeats, such as *kosisters*, *mebos*, *tamalatjes*, etc, and many a tummy-ache must have ensued among the younger generation, who usually gorged themselves to repletion.

The next event on the programme was the horseracing on the Greenpoint Common, which usually ended with a display of fireworks. Young people of today, with their varied amusements and entertainments, can scarcely imagine what an intense excitement these simple pleasures aroused in the people of those days, or how keenly they were anticipated and afterwards talked about.

The old Cape houses were built to suit the climate, and nearly all had spacious, open *stoeps*, many of which were built in the Italian style, with tall pillars or pergolas covered with trailing vines and creepers. It was the custom at the close of a hot day for the inmates of the houses to sit out on these stone-flagged *stoeps*. Family friends foregathered there to drink coffee, eat *konfyts*, and discuss the events of the day.

The fashionable café was a small shop in Burg Street kept by Miss Volstead, who was noted for her cakes and *konfyts*. This old lady—at least, I used to think her old—made wonderful sweetmeats and preserved fruits with equally wonderful names such as *gebrande amandel,*[1] *dumlaklontje*, *ublietjes*, and many other confections. Her marble-topped tables were kept scrupulously clean, and the scales and weights of polished brass shone like gold. When one entered the shop there was always a delicious smell of cinnamon and freshly-baked cakes, which I can recall to this day.

* * *

I must have turned my thoughts to money-making at an early age, for when I was ten or eleven years of age I used to earn a few shillings by taking watches out to ships lying in the Bay for a jeweller named

[1]. Burnt Almonds.

Williams, who had a shop in Adderley Street. He used to repair these watches for officers of the visiting ships. He was a dear old soul, a widower with a beautiful, fair, Christ-like face, and a mass of golden hair flecked with silver—very appropriate for a jeweller.

I was taken to the ships out in the Bay in one of the fishing-boats manned by a couple of Malays. If the wind was favourable we hoisted a sail, otherwise I was rowed out. Sometimes the sea was quite rough. I pride myself on the fact that I never failed to bring back to Williams the right payment that I was expected to receive, and the old gentleman, when he paid me my commission, was always very grateful to me for the services that I had rendered him.

Williams had a very pretty little daughter named Alice, and I dare say my admiration for her prompted me to render zealous service to her father. They lived in a house in Stael Plein, near Government House, opposite the present Botha Memorial.

Perhaps it was also because of Alice's *beaux yeux* that I was induced on one occasion to offer my services to Williams as a painter. The front hall of his house needed a coat of paint, and he offered me ten shillings if I would paint it for him. I told him I would have a try, and accordingly set to work with a brush and a pot of paint that Williams had bought. The result was not beautiful; the colour was as variegated as the hide of a zebra. However, Williams seemed to be satisfied, for he gave me my reward.

I remember the excavations and the buildings of the docks at Cape Town, though, of course, they have been enlarged and greatly improved since then. As boys my brother and I used to watch the convicts at work, and to us the work appeared to be a colossal piece of engineering. Later, from the deck of a tug in the Bay, we watched the christening ceremony. The docks were called after Prince Alfred, Duke of Edinburgh, second son of Queen Victoria, who in 1860 had paid his first visit to South Africa.

We were intrigued by this christening ceremony, especially the breaking of a bottle of champagne over the bows of the tug and the firing of salutes. There was a great display of bunting, and it was a gala occasion.

Prince Alfred's second visit to South Africa took place when I was about seven. He came out in command of HMS *Galatea*. He had with him as equerry the Hon Elliott Yorke, who was a very accomplished actor. My father, whose favourite hobby was amateur theatricals, organised a performance of *Richard the Third*, in which Yorke took one of the leading parts. My brother Bill and I made our first appearance before the footlights in the role of pages. I wore a pink satin suit, and had great pink rosettes on my shoes. I had my hair curled by the barber for the occasion, and felt very smart and extremely important, because I was allowed to remain in the men's dressing-room while Yorke and the others put on their costumes.

Rather to the consternation of the actors, Prince Alfred, with the Governor's wife on his arm, suddenly appeared at the door of the dressing-room.

From inside I had heard a woman's voice protesting, and the Prince's assurances that he knew the way. His idea was to surprise Yorke by suddenly throwing open the dressing-room door while the actors were making up. It was a little disconcerting, to say the least of it.

The performance took place in the Roman Catholic School, not far from the site of the present Cathedral, and as the play progressed I remember one of the scenes in which Richard was asleep in his tent. The man who took the part of Sir Richard Ratcliff had been told off to strike three times on his shield outside the King's tent, and when King Richard shouted, 'Zounds! Who is there?' Ratcliff had to say, 'Ratcliff, my lord: 'tis I, the early village-cock hath twice done salutation to the morn.' He evidently forgot his part. Looking in terror at the audience, he shouted, ''Tis I, m'lord, the early village-cock.' Greeted with boos from the back of the house, he turned and bolted off the stage.

When Prince Alfred left Cape Town he sailed along the coast, his next stop being Port Elizabeth. The whole town turned out to give him a royal welcome. The Mayor and Mayoress, Mr and Mrs Kettle, did all they could to give him a good time, and a banquet was given in his honour. Of course, he sat next to the Mayoress. All the guests seemed to have lost their tongues, few of them having ever seen a Royal prince before. Every word of the Prince's conversation was clearly heard in the general silence. Suddenly Mrs Kettle electrified the company by asking politely, 'How is your ma?' The Prince, though somewhat taken aback by this naïve remark, replied, 'Her Majesty was very well when I last heard of her.' He was then heard to ask the Mayoress, 'Are there any little Kettles?' To which she replied, 'Five little Kettles, three with spouts and two without.'

Whilst on his way to the Eastern Province the Prince passed through the Knysna Forest. In those days the country was very wild, with none of the roads which today enable tourists to see so much of the beautiful scenery, with its occasional glimpses of the sea through the gigantic forest trees. The Prince was anxious to shoot some wild game, and if possible an elephant.

At one of the halting-places, in a spirit of mischief, he mounted one of the horses and rode it bareback to the stream where the animals were to be watered. He was accompanied by one of the sailors from the *Galatea*.

After the horses had drunk their fill the Prince again mounted his steed and rode helter-skelter back to the camp at a mad gallop. This so terrified the sailor that he ran after the Prince, yelling, 'Hold hard, Your Royal Highness; if Your Royal Highness don't look out, Your Royal Highness will break his Royal bloody neck.'

The Prince thoroughly enjoyed his visit to South Africa, especially his shoot in the George district with his cousins the Rex family, and generally made himself very popular.

Chapter 2

The Discovery of Diamonds

It is difficult to describe the effect on the quiet and rather sleepy atmosphere of Cape Town produced by the discovery of diamonds in 1870 on the Vaal River and the New Rush. The New Rush was so called by Rawstone Kish and his party. Very soon people flocked from all parts of South Africa to the new field, and the veld was pegged off for miles. My father and brother Bill were among those who went in search of a fortune, and later on, in 1871, when the Colesberg Kopje Diamond Mine was found, they sent word to my mother and the rest of the family to join them.

We travelled by mule wagon from the Parade in Cape Town to the New Rush in one month; today the same journey by motor car takes one day. The impression left on my mind was that we were travelling all day and every day through a waterless and treeless country. We had to carry our water supply in small casks, and our fuel, which consisted of dry cow-dung, had to be collected at the outspans. The roads were mere wheel-tracks and the dust was appalling; the heat was terrible, the discomfort almost unendurable.

The roadside was strewn with the bodies of dead horses, mules, and oxen that had perished by the wayside; the stench was offensive. Vultures, the scavengers of the veld, were seen everywhere. We were never out of sight of game; springbok, blesbok, and wildebeeste were plentiful, but always a long way off. They had become very wild because of the continual traffic along the road.

The interior of the country was practically free from disease; rats, mosquitoes, and ticks being unknown, even on the diamond-fields. The advent of these plagues coincided with the coming of the transport wagons, which brought ticks and disease from the coastal areas of Natal, Port Elizabeth, and East London. As I have said, the country teemed with game of every kind, and once the traveller got away from the big towns he always had game in sight. In subsequent years, with the advance of railways and quicker means of locomotion, people spread over the land; moreover, breech-loading guns came into use, and much wild firing went on. Thus the game was steadily wiped out, and today one can travel from the Cape to the Zambesi and see comparatively few wild animals.

With the disappearance of wild animal life the carrion birds also vanished, and now, with the exception of the game reserves, where they are still to be found gloating over the remains of a lion's 'kill' and fighting with the jackals for the remnants of the feast, there are few vultures to be seen.

Those were surely the good old days, for there were no restrictions anywhere, wire fences being then unknown in South Africa. One could ride or drive across the country without hindrance. No licences to shoot were required, the whole world was one's own preserve, and fortunately the preserves were well stocked with game, for it was the only food obtainable beyond what one could carry.

It is difficult nowadays to get people to believe what a trek of game meant sixty years ago. I have seen fires made around the town grazing-lands of Victoria West and Boshof to prevent the buck from feeding on the pastures, which were needed for the cattle belonging to the residents of those *dorps*. Between Boshof and Bloemfontein I have seen herds of blesbok follow our mule wagon for miles; attracted by the trotting mules, they would canter up to within a hundred yards or less, and keep abreast of them. They were quite fearless.

Springbok, when disturbed, would invariably jump the road and then *pronk*, jumping high in the air and landing with all four feet bunched together. They would arch their backs and spread out a fan of snow-white hairs. They bounced up several times, then ran sideways, swerving and jumping in pure ecstasy of enjoyment, like kittens at play. Wildebeeste would form a wide circle and frisk round and round, gambolling and kicking up no end of dust. Colonies of meercats were so numerous that galloping across the veld was dangerous work, as the ground was a network of their holes. Ant-bears, porcupines, and rantle were very plentiful.

In the grass country which begins at the Modder River, oribi, duiker, and steenbok could be 'walked up' and killed by the score. The hills held *vaal* and *rooi* rhebok. Zebra were still quite plentiful in the Piquetberg and Clanwilliam districts, and bontebok were to be found in the Caledon area. Farther north hippos frequented Lake Chrissie in the Eastern Transvaal, and the Kaap valley round about Barberton was a paradise for hunters. To this day the bones of elephant may still be seen in Elephant's Creek on the bridle track between Barberton and Sheba.

Bird life was amazingly plentiful: the great imperial-crested bustard, several kinds of lesser *pauw*, korhaan, red-winged partridge, rock and tree partridge, pheasant, dikkop, hares, guinea fowl, and other game could be seen alongside of roads where there was little or no traffic; it was quite unnecessary to hunt for them.

Locusts were much more plentiful than they are today, and following the swarms of these insects were myriads of locust birds, a black and white species as large as a spreeu. These delightful and useful little birds moved about in dense columns performing the most wonderful manœuvres in the air. Rising like a whirlwind they would spiral up thousands of feet, forming a complete mass. Then they would drop to within a few feet of the ground, and skirmish in a line for twenty miles. They never seemed to alight. As long as the locusts flew on the birds would pursue them. Added to the lesser birds were red-legged storks and other large birds in great numbers, all feeding on the golden harvest.

* * *

At every farmhouse to which we came we heard complaints from the Boers of the treatment they had received from people passing on their way to the diamond-fields. They all demanded bread and water, and as the only water the farmers had was in the little dam near the homestead, and as bread was scarce because no grain crops were grown, these demands could not always be met. The water in the dams was polluted by the animals of the travelling teamsters, and many of the farmers were obliged to leave their homes because of the invasion. At one farm the windows had bullet-holes through them; a party of roughs had fired at the house because the owners had no bread to give them.

In spite of this the hospitality of the Boer was proverbial. I suppose I have travelled about South Africa as much as any man, but I cannot recall ever having been received discourteously by a Boer, or having met one who failed in hospitality. I have received more kindness from Boers than from any other race, and I have travelled the world over. True, I was able to speak their language, and I understood the customs of the country and complied with them.

The English, who were ignorant of the Dutch language and unable to adapt themselves to the conditions of a new, undeveloped country, were apt to be unreasonable, causing much bitterness and ill-feeling between the two peoples. The same may be said today, although racialism is largely kept alive for political purposes. There should really be no ill-feeling between Boer and Briton, because they have fought out their differences and have agreed to shake hands and be friends.

Those also who imagine that the people of Dutch origin are lacking in sportsmanship are entirely wrong. In all my long experience I have found no better sportsmen. They have supplied South Africa with some of her best cricket and football players; moreover, they can be chivalrous losers. During the Great War I had the opportunity of studying the young Afrikaans-speaking South Africans who came over to fight for the Empire. I was on reception committees and welfare and hospital committees, and I am glad to say that I was proud of these young men. They never grumbled, they were always polite, and they appreciated all that was done for them.

* * *

When eventually we arrived at Dutoitspan after our adventurous journey, our wagon was surrounded by a crowd of miners, who gave the ladies of our party three hearty cheers by way of welcome. Until then very few women had attempted the journey.

We soon began our life under canvas, and gradually became accustomed to dust, flies, and also to the lack of water, to say nothing of good food and all the other comforts that we had been used to at the Cape. It was a hard life, and it lasted for eight years. Everything had to be brought from the coast by ox or mule wagons, and we depended largely on tinned foods, which often caused ptomaine poisoning. Firewood cost £4 to £5 a load, mealie-meal cost £3 to £4 a *muid* sack, and the price of everything else was proportionately high.

My brother and I had to fetch our water supply from a well two miles distant from our camp. We inspanned ourselves to a small cask, the harness borne over our shoulders. The going was over very rough, stony veld, and when the hoops of the cask got loose we had to tighten them up with stones and stop the leakage with the pockets of our coats, which we tore off for that purpose. On arriving at our camp the cask was placed in a shady place, and our dog was chained to it to keep off the raiders.

The De Beers Mine, in fact the four mines that were known at that time, consisted of dead volcanic 'pipes.' The lava had come up from below through a comparatively small aperture in the basic rock thousands of feet below, and the so-called mine could be said to resemble an inverted cone. There was a limestone capping about five or six feet thick through which we had to dig in order to get at the diamondiferous ground below. It formed a sort of domed roof to the mine, and gave one the impression of a huge pot that had boiled over with a white froth on the top. The rims of these 'pipes,' as they were called, consisted of shale, except in the case of the De Beers Mine, whose rim was basaltic rock. The diamondiferous ground had been weathered down to about 200 feet in depth, and had changed its colour from a bluish hue to yellow. This yellow ground was fairly friable, and could be easily broken with a pick.

Diggers used to begin work at sunrise. When sufficient ground had been loosed, a rawhide bucket was filled and hauled to the surface by means of a crazy old wooden windlass and hemp rope. The ground was then tipped into a wheelbarrow and taken to the depositing floor, where it was dumped. It was a common sight to see Kaffirs sitting round the heap beating the lumps of this diamond-bearing ground with hardwood sticks, working in unison to the accompaniment of a monotonous song which corresponded in its tempo with the rise and fall of the blows.

SIFTING FOR DIAMONDS ON COLESBERG KOPJE
(AFTERWARDS NAMED KIMBERLEY) IN 1870

After the lumps had been broken up, the ground was passed through a sieve and put on a large iron-sheeted sorting-table. My job was to search the gravel for diamonds. For this purpose we used an iron scraper about nine inches long, made of strong hoop-iron held with a wooden handle. The gravel was spread out, a cupful at a time, and if there was no evidence of diamonds the ground was swept off by the scraper on to the ground. I had to keep my eyes skinned in order that the smallest stone might not be missed.

This was the simplest method we could adopt at the time, but in later years, when it became possible to break up the gravel by washing it with water, a great many more diamonds were found and our old tailings became very valuable.

By the time I had sorted a barrow-load another would come up from the mine, and so the work went on from sunrise to sunset. My only refreshment was supplied from a bottle of tepid water, which I concealed in a heap of rubble in the vain hope that it might keep cool. Luckily, our sorting-table was erected under a camel-thorn tree, and very grateful we were for even the flickering shade it afforded.

We were at that time working in the De Beers Mine, and our claims were in 'Poor Man's Gully.' The mine was in the first instance parcelled out into gullies—Australian Gully, Schwabs Gully, Poor Man's Gully, etc.

Our next-door neighbour was one of the few women in the camp—a Miss Swanepoel. She owned a claim, which she worked with the help of a few Kaffirs, from whom she rarely lifted her eagle eye, in case they might steal a diamond. She was a little wizened old spinster, and might have been of any age. She wore a huge *kappie*[1] lined with green stuff. She could hold her own with any man, and would stand no nonsense.

* * *

It was while sorting under the shade of my mimosa tree that I first saw Cecil Rhodes. He and Charles Rudd had a contract for pumping the water our of Baxter's Gully. Rhodes was then reading for his Oxford examinations, and used to go over from time to time to Oxford to keep his terms.

---

1. Linen sun-bonnet.

SIEVING AND SORTING AT THE KIMBERLEY DIAMOND MINE IN 1872

While he was working at his pumping contract he used frequently to come to our sorting-table to see what luck we had had. He was always asking us if we had found any diamonds. He used to pull out his scales and weigh and value the stones we had found, but he never bought any.

Sometimes he went over to Miss Swanepoel's claim, where he used to sit for hours chatting to her. He delighted in teasing her, but she was rewarded when he offered to weigh and value the stones she had found. Whenever afterwards he came to see her, he wanted to know if her stones had fetched the price which he had placed upon them.

As a rule he sat on the edge of the 'reef' which overlooked the mine, reading his books and listening to the pulsation of his pump. As long as the pump throbbed out its asthmatic beat in perfect regularity he went on reading, but when it stopped—which happened pretty frequently—he would hop down into the mine to see what was wrong, holding on to a rope with one hand and clutching his hat in the other. I remember the vision of him climbing down, with his fair hair blowing about in the wind.

Many other people used to come to our sorting-table to look on and gossip and ask us what we had found. Some used to offer to sell us cheap jewellery or exchange it for diamonds. Men like Sammy Marks and his partner, Isaac Lewis, who afterwards established themselves as prosperous financiers on the Rand, began their careers in this way.

Diamond sorting was weary work, especially as it was mostly unprofitable, but there were always elements of chance which spurred us on. Thus for a long time we fared very badly and had to struggle in our endeavour to make our claims pay.

At last one Saturday night we had come to the end of our tether. We had no money left, and we owed money at the local store; besides, the wages of our Kaffir boys for the week were due. We had cheerfully lived on mealie pap for some time, and were longing for a bit of meat. From early dawn on that eventful Saturday we had slogged away hoping for a little luck to pull us through.

I was sorting some ground when I noticed that it was of a different colour; it was dark green, richer looking, with garnets and carbon showing freely. I sprinted to the windlass and called down to my brother to 'stick it out,' for I was sure that we would find something in this new layer. He and my father were on the point of knocking off work, but, encouraged by me, they went on.

Barrow after barrow I sieved and sorted, but not a diamond was to be seen. It was getting late, and the Kaffirs were grumbling and wanted to go home to their *skoff*. As they swung their sticks in unison, breaking the lumps on our depositing-floor, they sang: '*Meena funa hamba khaya, meena funa skoff*.'[1]

I encouraged them to work on, promising them heaps of meat if we found anything. Just at that moment the barrow-boy tipped his last load on to the floor. Lo and behold, as he shot the stuff over, out rolled a beautiful big diamond! I made a grab at it and ran to the windlass, shouting down to the others to come out, and telling them what I had found.

We all went over, a very happy party, to Cotty's store that Saturday night. Groups of diggers were standing about, and when they heard of our luck they all cheered us and showered congratulations upon us. Our diamond was passed from hand to hand until quite fifty men must have examined it. Finally, we took it over to John Burbeck's office. He was a diamond buyer, and he weighed the stone for us. It was what is called a frosted Cape-white, and weighed 32½ carats.

As dusk began to fall, having purchased our stores and much meal and meat for the Kaffirs, a happy singing procession returned to the camp, greatly rejoicing. Eventually J B Robinson, who was both a digger and diamond buyer, bought the stone from us for £750.

---

1. 'We want to go home, we want our food.'

Chapter 3

How We Lived on the Diamond Diggings

Life in the early days of the diamond-fields was full of stirring incidents. Imagine about ten thousand white people and about three times as many Kaffirs, all living in various-shaped tents scattered over the area now occupied by the town of Kimberley, and having to cook their food in the open air.

Every day the clouds of dust grew denser and the mine ground, when broken up, filled the air with additional dust, which, after rain, turned into mud. Each thunderstorm was introduced by a hurricane of wind, which covered everything with a thick layer of sand.

As time went on more diggers arrived, more soil was broken and sifted, and the whole camp assumed a dirty-white appearance. Picture a 'digger' party, returning to camp at sunset, dusty, dry and worn out, having toiled all day in the broiling sun, to find that the wind had blown down their tents, and left all their bedding and cooking outfits covered with an inch of filth.

No sooner would all hands have fixed up the tents and got things straight, when down would come a torrential shower of rain or hail accompanied by thunder and lightning. By the time the storm had passed and the bedding had been cleaned, most of the weary men would go to bed supperless, any cooking for them being out of the question. Those

RIVER DIGGINGS AT KLIPDRIFT, 1870

who luckily had 'boys' to cook for them or wives to fend for them fared better, but the majority of the men depended in such an emergency on tinned food, if they had any.

Water at first was very scarce, obtainable in sufficient quantity for drinking purposes only. When, however, more water was found in the mine as the excavations became deeper, we were able to wash the pulverised ground instead of having to sieve it dry.

I think it was an Australian who introduced the 'Long Tom,' which consisted of a long, shallow box fixed on a slope. Upon this the mine ground was dumped and washed with a stream of water which carried away the clay and pulverised lime, leaving the rubble behind. This rubble was then put into a large circular sieve, which was jigged up and down in a tub full of water. Thus the heavier particles accumulated at the bottom, so that when the sieve was finally turned bottom upward on the sorting-table, any diamonds that there might be in the material were easily visible lying on the top.

Some people used a 'Rocker' instead of the 'Long Tom,' but the jigging of the washed material in the sieve was the common practice.

When later on the 'blue' unweathered ground was encountered at depth in the mine, many diggers lost heart and either sold their claims at very low prices or even abandoned them entirely. Working had become by that time very expensive owing to the high cost of material and labour; moreover, the workings had become too deep for hand-hauling. The price of diamonds had also fallen.

It was then that small companies were formed to acquire blocks of claims. These companies were afterwards amalgamated into larger concerns until the final unification of the whole diamond industry was effected under the control of Cecil Rhodes, Alfred Beit, and Barney Barnato.

* * *

Those who were lucky enough to possess horses and carts could go to the Vaal River on Sundays for a bathe; the less fortunate ones had to foot it to Klipdrift—a twenty-mile tramp each way under a burning sun. The journey was anything but pleasant, but the yearning for a bathe and a good soak in the river was so great that we used to go to Klipdrift after knocking off work on a Saturday, returning on the Sunday. We usually selected moonlit nights for the trip.

During one weekend we were the guests of Mr Piet Volstead, who lived at Klipdrift on the river, where he made beer. When we came in to breakfast on the Sunday morning, my brother Bill sat down and stretched out his legs. Suddenly he shouted, 'By God, there's a snake crawling up my leg!' The women in the room got up and fled; it was just as well, because my father seized hold of Bill's trousers and dragged them off. Right down near his feet was a poor little duckling that had crawled up his trousers looking for crumbs, and could not get out!

*   *   *

As long as the weather was fine life under canvas was happy enough—but oh, those storms! I have mentioned them before, but I must mention them again because they were the bugbear of our lives. During the summer months, usually at about 4 pm, we could see what looked like a black bank on the horizon, foretelling a storm. Then we would run to our tents and tighten the ropes, pegging down the sides and making everything snug. Preceded by the usual cloud of red dust, the gale would sweep over Colesberg Kopje, where 20 000 miners were sieving. Soon it became impossible to see more than a yard ahead; then the thunder crashed, and down came a torrential deluge. In a few minutes half an inch of rain would fall, and everything would be soaked; then the clouds would roll by, the sun shone brightly again, and out we came from our shelters to see what damage the storm had done. Everywhere tents were lying flat, and the mess inside was indescribable. What a life!

On one occasion I was returning to the camp, having retrieved my pony from the flats at De Beers, when I ran into one of these storms. I took shelter in a digger's tent and helped him to hold up the pole to prevent the wind from blowing the tent down. The digger's family were sitting on the ground, crouching in terror of the storm, which was at that moment particularly fierce. It was one of the worst storms I have ever been in, with heavy rain and hail interspersed with terrific claps of thunder, and with lightning striking all round us. I remember that, while all this was going on, one of the little children went down on her knees and rested her elbows on a soap-box. She put her hands together and raised her eyes to heaven, and, in the most reverent manner, said, 'O Lord, for what we are going to receive may the Lord make us truly thankful.'

* * *

At twelve years of age I found myself driving a mule team, carting diamondiferous ground from the mine to our sorting-floor. My father owned one-quarter of a claim in No 1 Road in the Kimberley Mine, and it was being worked by Isaac Robinson and Willie McPherson, whom I was sent to help.

Willie McPherson was a great character, and there were many stories told about him.

On one occasion he was walking down the street in Kimberley carrying a white woollen bag of 'giant' gunpowder. He was smoking Boer tobacco, and some red-hot ashes had fallen on the bag, which began to smoulder. People shouted to him, 'Look out, your gunpowder's alight!' Without any hesitation he calmly flicked the red-hot ash away with his finger and went on smoking.

After a lapse of sixty years, I was reminded by Willie McPherson how I had driven the mule team for them. In his later years Willie was the pound-master at Barberton. He died in 1936, and before he died he wrote me a letter reminding me of the old Kimberley days.

* * *

For some years there were no fixed laws on the diamond-fields, and men did not know whether they owed allegiance to Her Majesty's Government or to the Orange Free State. The miners therefore often took the law into their own hands and meted out very severe punishment to anyone found stealing or buying stolen diamonds.

On one occasion a man owning a canteen in the west end of the New Rush was suspected of having bought stolen diamonds from Kaffirs, and as it was said that a case had been proved against him the miners decided to burn him out. Word was passed round, and as the miners knocked off work they moved in a body towards the canteen and made it clear to the proprietor what they intended to do. Without a moment's hesitation the canteen-keeper climbed the tent-pole and sat across the ridge of the tent. From there he harangued the crowd.

'Boys,' said he, 'I'm a family man and my wife and children are inside. I'm innocent; I never bought diamonds from anyone; this is a trumped-up charge, and you'll regret what you're going to do. If you're going to burn my place down I'll burn with it. Go on, do your damnedest—I don't care!'

Some of the crowd shouted, 'You are a damned liar!' The majority, however, wavered. Perhaps, after all, the man might be innocent. They began to look foolishly at one another, as much as to say, 'What the devil are we going to do now?' It was evident that the canteen-keeper had won. Suddenly one of the ringleaders shouted, 'Haul him down, boys!' But the crowd had begun to melt away. They were not absolutely satisfied, but they decided to let the man off for the sake of his wife and children.

* * *

In the 'seventies the Karroo was not heavily grazed, and the condition of the veld was therefore much better than it is now. I may be wrong, but I fancy that the rainfall was greater then than it is now, and my reason for thinking so is that the pans were often full of water for two or three seasons in succession.

The shooting round about Kimberley was always very good, and so was the coursing; it was because there was plenty of food and cover in the Vaal bushes for buck and hares. We also used to shoot snipe over some of the large pans near the town. Painted snipe were quite common. Egyptian geese, duck, spur-winged geese, and many kinds of wild-fowl were plentiful on these pans, but they were all very shy. Some of the large pans were five or six miles in circumference, and in the rainy season held about three to four feet of water. There were always large swarms of locusts and flying-ants, upon which the wild-fowl fed.

In winter, about 8 am, sand-grouse in thousands would come to the pans to drink; rock-pigeon would come at dawn, but as they were too shy and easily alarmed, we never got many of them. There was, however, no limit to the number of sand-grouse, and they were easy to shoot because they were so keen on quenching their thirst that they kept returning within easy range, piping their cry of '*Kelke-wyn, Kelke-wyn*' in their flight.

An amazing phenomenon, and one over which I have since puzzled, took place during the rains. I have seen a small pan that had been as dry as a bone, with the mud bottom as hard as iron, fill overnight, and in the morning on the surface there would be scores of water-tortoises swimming about. Whence they came I have never known. It was quite impossible that they could have been hidden in the mud, because any mud that lay on the hard slate bottom was barely deep enough to cover the tortoises, each of which must have weighed about two pounds.

* * *

Visitors to the Kimberley Mine today look down on a vast circular hole, immense in circumference, but few remember the opening scenes of the digging of that great hole. A mining claim was 30 feet by 30 feet, and each was sometimes split into eighths, and worked by individuals. In time, as the claims were worked down, roadways had to be left, by which the diamondiferous ground was carted out; ox-carts, mule-carts, wheelbarrows, and hand-barrows being used for the purpose. For some time, along No 6 Road, a little mule was used for drawing a cart; I remember this mule distinctly because she was such an active little thing. They called her 'Busy Bee,' and every man in the mine knew her well.

Later, the roadways fell in and the mine had to be worked by high gears and windlasses from the banks above. The scene always reminded me of a great beehive: whites and blacks swarmed in the claims; buckets flew up and down the aerial ways, and a hum of voices contributed to the din.

Every now and again a landslide would take place, and then ten thousand voices would send up a rousing shout mingled with whistling and screeching on native musical instruments. Then a band of Kaffirs fresh from their homes would issue shrill cries from all over the mine; there would be more whistling, more noise from native tom-toms, more shouts.

At knock-off time our Kaffirs used to pass down streets of tented shops owned by white traders and presided over by yelling black salesmen, whirling guns above their heads. These they discharged in the air, crying

'*Reka Reka*, *Mona Mtsheka*.' A deafening din. A sight never to be forgotten. The small storekeepers used, in those days, to bring up wagon-loads of antiquated muzzle-loading rifles for sale to the Kaffirs, who frequently were met along the road proceeding to their homes armed to the teeth. An old gun, a canister of powder, a bar of lead, and a bullet-mould constituted glorious equipment for robbing and killing white people.

Chapter 4

School in Natal

In 1873 my parents, anxious that I should have some schooling, sent me to Natal. I travelled there by mule wagon in company with Jonke Ferreira, who some years later was killed at Kamboola in the Zulu war by a spent bullet which hit him in the forehead while he was standing on a wagon watching the retreat of the Zulus.

Passing through the Free State we were never out of sight of game; blesbok, mistaking our mules for trek-bok, would join us and follow for miles quite close to the wagon, when the drivers would scare them away by cracking their whips.

My destination was Greytown, where my uncle, named Peter Hellet, lived. He was a brother of my mother, and a great friend of Louis Botha, the father of the renowned General Botha. My uncle had married Annie Botha, the General's eldest sister. He was very kind to me, and sent me to a school conducted by a German Mission at Hermansberg, about eighteen miles from Greytown. It was then the best school in Natal and J B Lindley, George Moor, and many other well-known Natalians were educated there.

When I was at school I used sometimes to go out hunting with a lot of little Zulu boys. We all carried throwing-sticks, which we hurled at hares or partridges, or anything else that we flushed. We formed a long half-moon and went through the long grass in that way. If a covey of partridges rose, twenty or more sticks from all angles would hurtle into their midst, often bringing a bird down.

In walking through the long grass one is always liable to tread on a snake. I remember that I was once crossing a little path when a puff-adder struck at me, but the instant before one of the Zulu boys who was with me had shouted '*N'yoga*,' and I had jumped the right way and avoided the blow.

A little later we saw some crows' nests in a tree. I climbed up to get the eggs, and on putting my hand into the nest I found a snake known as a *boomslang* coiled up in it.

* * *

Boys in my young days were much more independent and self-reliant than they are today. Our small aches and pains did not meet with much sympathy. For instance, while I was at school a hollow tooth was giving me a very bad time, and one of the bigger boys advised me to destroy the nerve with a red-hot wire; so I stuck one end of a hair-pin in a cork, made the other end red hot, and jammed it into the tooth. Then the fun began! The throbbing pain was as regular as the ticking of a clock. The agony was so unbearable that I went to the headmaster and asked leave to go to Greytown, eighteen miles away, to have the tooth out. It was nine o'clock at night, and he said it was much too late for me to go. However, I persisted, and eventually was given permission. Off I started. It was a cold, starlit winter's night, and I had some distance to go along a Kaffir footpath before I struck the Helpmekaar road.

By the time I reached the road I saw a big grass fire approaching. It was a long way off, but the wind was fairly strong and there was just a chance that I might be caught. I stepped out briskly, almost forgetting the pain I was suffering, so great was my fear of being trapped by the fire.

After plodding along for some miles the fire began to get dangerously near me, and all sorts of animals crossed the road fleeing from the intense heat. I could hear screaming birds on the wind; buck and even a tortoise were among the escaping creatures of the veld. It became very hot, the smoke was suffocating, and the flames were spreading at an alarming pace. There was nothing for it but to run, and run I did—I must have made a world record. When I was almost exhausted I came by good luck to a stream, and that saved me.

I reached Greytown about daybreak, went straight to Dr B's house, and rang the bell. The doctor opened the door, and when I told him that I wanted him to pull out one of my teeth, he was furious and asked me what I meant by waking him up at that hour of the morning. As he had shut the door in my face, I sat down on the doorstep and waited patiently until he had finished his breakfast. After that he came out to see me in a more amiable mood and took me into his surgery. There he pulled out my tooth, and then and there I vowed that I would take care of my teeth from that day forward. This I did so well that I had no trouble with them for thirty years.

I spent most of my school holidays with my relations, the Mennes, who owned a belt of country along the Umvoti River, where my grandmother, Mrs Hellet, had settled. Her maiden name had been Maria Cornelia Bandel. In 1820 she had married Johan Pieter Hellet, who was of Danish origin and had arrived in the Cape at the beginning of the nineteenth century as captain of a British ship. He settled in Cape Town and was the owner of several cargo-boats, which plied between the shore and the ships in the roadstead. He was a man of great energy, and owned a number of slaves. When he died in 1840 he left my grandmother to carry on his business as well as she could. When the British Government decided to release all the slaves in the Cape Colony she, in common with all the other slave owners, received by way of compensation merely a money order, which could only be cashed in London. As this order had to be presented by the payee in person, and as she could not go to London, she was unable to obtain any redress for the loss of her slaves. This nearly ruined her. Most of the slave-owners in the Colony suffered in the same way, and it was partly owing to this unjust treatment that several families shook the dust off their feet and followed in the wake of the Great Trek to the north.

My grandmother decided to settle in Natal, and in 1862 she sailed by a coasting vessel to Durban with her three children, William, Peter and Hendrika. Her eldest daughter, Johanna, had in 1844 married Theodore Menne, and while they decided to go overland to Natal with five of their smaller children, my grandmother agreed to take five of their elder children with her by sea.

As I have already recorded, my grandmother's eldest son, Peter Hellet, when he grew to manhood, settled in Greytown and married General Botha's eldest sister. He was highly respected, and after his death a monument in his memory was erected in the town gardens of Greytown.

One of my grandmother's slaves named Machumar remained a faithful servant all his life. He refused to be emancipated, and begged to be allowed to accompany her in the ship to Natal. He was a great character and we all liked him, for he was very kind to all of us youngsters. Every Sunday morning he dressed himself up in an old blue naval coat with epaulettes, white-duck trousers, and white cotton gloves, and paraded backwards and forwards before the house.

In trekking across the Free State into Natal, my Aunt Johanna with her husband, Theodore Menne, accompanied by some of their children, had a very strenuous journey. In those days hardships were taken as they came. For instance, my aunt gave birth to twins when they were journeying towards Winburg in the Orange Free State.

Her husband, Theodore, had been born in Germany and, after travelling to Holland, finally decided to immigrate to North America. Owing to contrary winds his ship was driven into Rio de Janeiro in South America. As he did not fancy settling in that country, he decided to take ship for the Cape of Good Hope. There he became great friends with the Hellet family, and in 1844, on one of his visits to the Cape, he married my Aunt Johanna. He had a considerable knowledge of farming, trading in stock, which he put to good account by buying sheep and cattle up-country and selling them in the Cape. His journeys took him all over the country as far as the northern extremities of the Transversal, and his wife frequently accompanied him.

For a time he settled in Natal and bought the farm *Cedara*, which is now the Government School of Agriculture. After paying a visit to Germany, he returned to the Cape and bought a lot of property near Sir Lowry's Pass, Gordon's Bay and Hangklip, where he engaged in wine and cereal farming.

He must have been a great rover, for in 1865 he went back to Natal, where he purchased many farms in the Umvoti county, in all about 11 000 acres. He there built himself a house, which he christened *Menneheim*, and eventually died in 1905.

Sad to relate, my uncle, Peter Hellet, died suddenly in 1875, and I was sent back to the diamond-fields. Old Louis Botha happened to be taking his daughter Sophie home. This gave me the chance of a lift in his wagon as far as Harrismith. From there I caught the post-cart and travelled to Kimberley with James Grice of Durban and his sister, both of whom were very kind to me.

On my return to Kimberley I immediately started work again sorting diamonds; we were then working a claim belonging to Duncan and Dunsmuir on shares. We had a block of claims in the De Beers Mine, which we found very difficult to hold because of the licence money and a new mining regulation which had to be complied with. The Claim Inspectors demanded that the ground be worked to the level of our neighbours' ground in order to make it safe. Unfortunately there happened to be a blank layer of some fifty feet, which was dead ground containing no diamonds. This eventually ruined us; and in order to help my family, I took a job as salesman with E W Tarry at £15 a month.

Tarry was in the hardware business, and the firm still exists. The bookkeeper was one Charles Downing, who was a hard drinker but a very likeable fellow. In order that he might take an occasional day off, he taught me bookkeeping and found me so apt a pupil that when he died I kept Tarry's books until a qualified man could be found.

The open-air life we led under rough conditions made us very hardy. Whenever possible we made expeditions into the country, taking our guns with us and frequently bringing home our dinner. On one of these occasions Fred St Leger and I were returning to our camp shortly after sunset. We had kept our guns loaded on the chance of another shot, when suddenly Fred blazed off right across my chest, and swore he had blown the head off a huge yellow cobra that had reared to strike me.

I had not seen the snake, and did not believe him; he was, however, so positive and persisted in arguing about it that, as it was growing dark, I hung my handkerchief on a bush nearby to mark the place. On the following morning we went to look for the snake; and there, right enough, was the cobra at the entrance of an ant-bear hole with its head blown almost clean off.

When I was a few years younger, I had had a narrow escape. I had a friend, the son of Dr Reitz of the Dutch Reformed Church, who was the Minister at Somerset West. The boy's name was Basie, and he was

THE DIAMOND MARKET AT KIMBERLEY IN 1888
ALFRED BEIT'S OFFICE IS ON THE EXTREME LEFT

four or five years older than I. Being a keen sportsman, he taught me to shoot, and I used to follow him about like a dog, carrying his powder, shot and knapsack. On one of our excursions to the spot where the De Beers Explosives Factory now stands, Basie and I had to jump across a ditch five or six feet wide. He told me to go first and that he would hand the gun across to me. Over I went, and as I landed Basie shouted, '*Koes*, Jimmy!'[1] As I crouched he fired and killed a big yellow cobra a foot or two from me.

* * *

The country round about the Umvoti in Natal was infested with snakes. When in 1882 I was on a visit to my uncle, Theodore Menne, at Menneheim, I was returning home after a day's shooting and had to pass along a row of fig trees. I pulled down a branch to get some ripe figs, and felt something hit me on the thigh. Thinking it was a branch that had been released and had struck me, I was not alarmed till I heard the angry hiss of a snake. I could just see his head, and I took a snap shot at him and managed to get him. I had on a very long canvas shooting-coat with an all-round pocket in which to put game. In it were a couple of duck and some snipe, and they probably saved my life, for the broken fang of the snake and a spot of poison were found sticking in the coat.

This reminds me of another escape I had from death. Once I was stalking some duck on the Schoenspruit, near Ventersdorp, and I had a pointer with me. As I crawled along in the long grass—putting the gun down first and crawling up to it—my dog drew ahead and snarled. I thought he had sighted an iguana, but I took the precaution to draw my gun back. As I did so a black cobra rose a foot away from me, but fortunately it was looking at the dog. I managed to blow his head off, but the shock had the effect of making me violently sick.

There were so many snakes around Schoenspruit that on another occasion when I was out shooting guinea fowl, a yellow cobra struck me in the leg; fortunately I had big top boots on and I shot him before he could strike again.

I could tell of many experiences of hairbreadth escapes of this kind, for in those days snakes were plentiful, and my wandering all over South

---

1. 'Crouch, Jimmy.'

Africa took me into places where it was very likely that I might come across them.

To anyone keen on shooting, as I have always been, there was always the risk of a fatal snakebite, and one had to keep a constant lookout. A bite from a venomous snake frequently meant almost instantaneous death, as in those days there were no anti-venom serums such as can now be bought at most chemists' shops. What risks we ran!

Generally speaking, I found that snakes and wild animals always fled from mankind and were rarely aggressive. I cannot say, however, that I have found that the same remark applies to venomous insects. Dick Rimer and I once pegged off a block of claims on what is now the Wesselton Mine. We pitched our small prospector's tent, which was only about four feet high, on our claims, and waited for a capitalist to come along and buy us out.

On the second night of our occupation I was awakened by the braying of our donkey. It was bright moonlight; every stitch in the canvas over our heads could be plainly seen. Imagine my horror when I saw crawling over the tent scores of scorpions! There they were, running backwards and forwards! Many of them were small, but there were one or two real whoppers among them. They seemed very excited, and fearing that they might prospect inside the tent, I awakened Dick, and we made a bolt for it.

It was a cold night, so we decided to light a fire, but the only fuel we could find was damp cow dung, which gave forth more smoke than heat. Hunched up over the smoke, Dick and I sat till daylight. As soon as we could see we crept warily up to the tent, picking up stones with which we intended to smash the scorpions. Not one could be seen! Nevertheless, nothing could have persuaded us to spend another night on those claims, which we gladly abandoned.

Chapter 5

Journeys into the Interior

At seventeen years of age I began to get restless, and frequently, whenever I could afford the time, I used to take my gun and necessary kit and go off on some 'voyage of discovery.'

Once I went up the Vaal River shooting, as far as Parys, and then on to Kroonstad, taking with me a Berthon collapsible boat. In order to get to the river from Kimberley I struck across the country *via* Bloemhof. I had a friend with me, and we had a wonderful time. *En route* we passed through a farm owned by one of the Stowes of Kimberley. When we reached the house I knocked at the front door, but no one answered although I made a lot of noise.

I then pushed open the top half of the door, and, to my horror, a huge yellow cobra reared up in the middle of the room. Whilst we hunted for something with which to kill the snake, Stowe turned up and wanted to know what all the excitement was about.

'Excitement,' I said. 'Look at that snake!'

'Oh,' said he, 'that's Tommy, my tame snake. He's all right, just leave him alone.'

He told us that he had reared the snake, and made a pet of it!

Two months later on our return journey we passed through Stowe's farm again, but this time I came up to the house with great caution lest the snake might be about. However, Stowe came out at that moment and assured us that the coast was clear.

As a matter of fact he had killed the snake. He told us that one cold night it had crawled into his bed for warmth, and that as he wasn't sure whether it was 'Tommy' or not, he had killed it so as to be on the safe side.

* * *

Another trip I took towards the end of 1878 was with a trader called Bill Finnaughty, who was travelling with his wagon full of native 'trade stuff' into the country beyond Kuruman.

From the Hartz River, as we trekked northward, the whole country was alive with game, and we had no difficulty in keeping our camp supplied with meat.

The native petty chiefs through whose territory we passed were very independent and arrogant. One evening we arrived at a watering place near a large native *kraal*. We had just outspanned and were thinking of cooking our supper before turning in, when a native boy rode up to our wagon with an impertinent message from his chief to the effect that unless Finnaughty gave him brandy and powder he would send his people to turn us out of his country.

My friend Finnaughty was at that moment sitting at the back of the wagon cleaning his rifle. He had heard what the boy said, but he went on with his work without looking up. When he had finished, he slowly slipped a cartridge into the rifle and took leisurely aim at a small black and white bird that had alighted on an ant-heap fifty or sixty yards away. The next thing the native saw were the remains of the bird blowing away in the wind.

'Go, boy, back to your master, and tell him that is my answer,' was all he said.

Needless to say, we were not molested after this, but spent a peaceful night before continuing our journey northward.

We had intended to make our way into Matabeleland, but on the way we learnt that Lobengula, the great Matabele chief, was refusing to allow people to enter his country without permission. We soon found this to be correct, for just as we had crossed the border we found ourselves surrounded by an *impi* of Lobengula's warriors, who said that they had instructions to turn us back, and we were reluctantly obliged to abandon our journey.

No sooner had we returned to Kimberley than the Cape Government called for volunteers to quell a rebellion led by two Griquas, Donkin Malgaas and Jantjie. Their following consisted of Hottentots and Griquas. These rebel forces roamed about the country robbing and murdering storekeepers. Men and women were brutally butchered and all their property was destroyed. They killed the Burnette family, and Thompson, the father of Rhodes's friend, who was known as 'Matabele Thompson,' because of the leading part he took in 1873 in obtaining for Rhodes the historic concession over Lobengula's territory between the Limpopo and the Zambesi.

These murders excited so much resentment at that time that I, with several other young men, joined up at once under the command of Colonel Charles Warren and Major Owen Lanyon, who were both subsequently knighted. The chief stronghold of the rebels was in the Langeberg Mountains. Among the organised bodies of volunteers serving under the British flag were the Kimberley Light Horse, the Kimberley Artillery, and the Kimberley Infantry.

I belonged to the Artillery, and although we had no guns we went to the front as infantrymen with old Lancaster smooth-bore rifles that could not be depended upon to kill at a hundred yards. The ammunition was very old, and the outfit quite useless for Kaffir warfare. When Griquatown was besieged we went to the relief of that town, and afterwards fought engagements at Gomeperi, Lataku, and on the mountain heights of the Langeberg, driving the rebels before us into the desert and looting their cattle.

* * *

Having once got the taste for travel, I seized every opportunity that gave me a chance of seeing something of the hinterland, tales of which filtered through to Kimberley as hunters returned from the north. Thus it came about that when a retired naval officer called Gus Fisher, who had come to South Africa to seek a cure for lung trouble, asked me to join him in a trading expedition to the Spelonken in the Northern Transvaal, I jumped at it.

This was in 1879, when British troops were engaged in subduing Cetewayo, King of the Zulus.

When everything was ready, we made an early start on a beautiful morning. We had a comfortable tented-wagon, sixteen good oxen, and two excellent Kaffir boys.

As we neared Marico, we came across a beautiful pool of crystal-clear water about twelve feet deep. It looked so tempting that we decided to have a swim.

As soon as we had undressed I suggested to Gus that he should throw in a sixpence and let me dive for it. I rather think that he suspected that it would be the last he'd see of his sixpence. However, he threw it in and I dived in after it.

I had to go nearly to the bottom before I grabbed the coin, and my lungs were nearly bursting when I rose, struggling, to the surface.

Just at that moment I looked up. There was a beastly green mamba snake swimming just over my head; he had evidently been lying under cover of the bank, waiting for a frog to appear. My splash had apparently terrified him, and he had darted across the water to get to his hole.

I thought my last hour had come, but luckily my head just missed the snake. Needless to say, I didn't have another dive.

Gus was possessed, as most sailors are, of a nautical almanac, and it happened that on the day on which we were passing the village of Ventersdorp in the Western Transvaal, an eclipse of the sun was due. We had outspanned close to a large *kraal*, and we strolled over to have a chat with the headman.

Gus nudged me and said, 'Tell him that much blood will flow today in Zululand, that many will be killed, and that the god of the white people will draw a veil over the sun so that he may not see the slaughter and great bloodshed.'

No sooner had I translated his words than the eclipse actually commenced. It almost seemed that a miracle had taken place. Cries of wonder went up on all sides, the women throwing their blankets over their heads and running to their huts. We could hear the Kaffirs talking half the night.

Early the next morning we inspanned at dawn and trekked on northwards without any further excitement, until we neared the Elands River, where we came upon a camp occupied by some Boers.

I remember this place well, because they showed us the spoor of numerous snakes that had passed their camp on the previous day, also the skins of half a dozen they had killed. I had never heard of a trek of snakes before. It may have been a veld fire that had driven them that way. What astonished me was that the spoor covered all sorts and sizes of snakes from python to cobra.

* * *

When Gus Fisher and I were returning from our trading expedition we outspanned at about twenty miles from Ventersdorp, when we came across a Boer of the name of Niemand. He wore sandals of his own making, without socks. The extraordinary thing about him was that he had no fear of any kind of snake. He told us that the Bible had taught him 'to tread on the head of the viper and crush it with your heel.' This he never hesitated to do, however deadly the snake happened to be.

If he saw a snake go into a hole or into a crevice of a wall, he would seize it by the tail, pull it out and give it a swing round his head, cracking it like a whip. This broke its spine, when he would throw it on the ground and stamp on its head with his heel.

He claimed to have the poison of all the various kinds of snakes that abounded in the district, and he said that he doctored himself if ever he were bitten by a snake.

It was at the same place that a heavy storm came on, and we had to draw the tarpaulin over the wagon in order that we might partake of our midday meal in comparative comfort.

Just as we were settling down to eat, a Boer came along the road in a wagon drawn by sixteen oxen. As the storm broke he halted his wagon and took shelter under the covered portion. The storm lasted some time, with much thunder and lightning. After a while, the rain stopped and we heard to Boer calling out to his Kaffir to take the *trek-tou* and start away leading the foremost oxen. We lifted up our tarpaulin to see what was happening, and saw the Boer with one foot on the step and another on the front board of his wagon, ready to proceed on his journey.

He was in the act of cracking his whip when there was a blinding flash of lightning, followed by a deafening peal of thunder. So vivid was the flash that it blinded us for a few seconds. To our horror we saw, where there had been sixteen oxen, only one front and one aft ox standing up. The remainder had been killed by the flash.

The poor man had been killed and flung some yards away from the wagon, but the native boy was only stunned. The only thing we could do was to take his body into Ventersdorp.

On our way to the village we passed the native *kraal* where we had outspanned on our journey northward.

To our astonishment we were met by a deputation of natives singing our praises and offering us gifts. They appeared to look upon us with superstitious awe.

They told us that we had, on our previous visit, spoken truly; that the god of the white people had surely known that the Zulus were slaughtering the white soldiers when he drew a veil over the sun so that he might not see the bloodshed.

From what we could gather from their chatter, a great battle, afterwards known as the battle of Isandhlwana, had been fought in Zululand, and it was rumoured that the army of the white people had been wiped out.

The next morning early we made tracks for Kimberley as quickly as we could travel.

When we arrived we found that the success attained by Cetewayo, King of the Zulus, over the British forces had caused much unrest among the other Kaffir tribes. For instance, Gasibone, the Paramount Chief of the Batlapin tribe, had revolted. When I say that he was Paramount Chief, I mean that he had been, and still claimed to be, but that the British Government had deposed him and set up Morkerene as Chief in his place. Great excitement arose, and Gasibone and his followers went into rebellion, raiding farms and stealing cattle. This led to instructions being issued to Colonel Owen Lanyon, the administrator of Griqualand West, to call for volunteers to quell the revolt. I joined the mounted infantry, but as they gave us no uniform we wore corduroys. It was a bloodless affair, because at our approach the Kaffirs fled to their stronghold at Pokwani. We seized their cattle and burnt their huts, took some prisoners, and then returned to Kimberley.

The Chief, Gasibone, fled to his mountains, and from his hiding place sent a messenger to Kimberley asking Piet Buyskes, a well-known lawyer of that town, to come and see him with the object of hearing his complaint and laying it before the Queen of England. His message stated that he had not wanted to fight the English and that he had not fired a shot, although his *kraal* had been destroyed. Buyskes accepted the Chief's invitation and asked me to go with him as a guide. I gladly offered my services.

After a strenuous trek in a Cape cart drawn by six mules we reached the spot indicated by the messenger as the place where the Chief and his counsellors were encamped. It was in the hilly country beyond Pokwani. Gasibone had about two hundred of his followers with him.

As I got out of the cart I heard murmurs all round me, and I could see that I had been recognised by my corduroy coat as having been a member of the expedition which had fought against the Chief. It was a very awkward moment for me, because the counsellors began to take up a threatening attitude towards me. They had already commenced gesticulating and shouting.

One old Kaffir was particularly hostile towards me. I recognised him at once as the man whom, during the fight, I had dragged out of an ant-bear hole into which he had crawled with his kieries, assegais and an old muzzle-loader gun. When the old warrior saw me he began clamouring loudly for my blood, whereupon Buyskes, to whom I had told the story of my previous encounter with the old man, held up his hand and asked the Chief to call his men to order.

When all was quiet Buyskes said, 'Gasibone, if you were to tell one of your men to do a thing and he refused to do it, what would you do?'

Gasibone thereupon drew his finger across his throat, saying, 'I would kill him.'

Then Buyskes, pointing at me in a dramatic manner, said, 'This man was sent by his Queen to fight against you. He had to obey or he would have been killed. However, in order to show that he had no feeling against you or your people, he brought me here so that your grievances could be enquired into. As far as this man is concerned,' he said, pointing to the old warrior, 'my friend, when he was with the soldiers who fought against you, happened to find him hiding in an ant-bear hole!' [Loud jeers.] 'He did not hurt the old man, but as you see he released him.'

To be given away like that before his companions was too much for the old soldier, who slunk away and gave us no more trouble.

A *pitsu*[1] then took place, attended by Gasibone and his headmen, and, after a few days' palaver, Buyskes was fully posted with his instructions for his mission to England.

Just as we were preparing to return to Kimberley, there arrived a messenger from the Transvaal with a note from Paul Kruger[2] to Buyskes. The message was to the effect that as Kruger had learned that Buyskes was going to England on behalf of Chief Gasibone, he would be much obliged if Buyskes could manage to come to Rustenburg in the Transvaal and meet him because he wanted Buyskes to present the case of the Boer people to the British Government at the same time. The letter stated that the Boers were very dissatisfied with the way in which the British Government had robbed them of their country, and went on to say that if it were not returned to them they would go into rebellion.

Buyskes looked at me and asked me whether I would accompany him. I consented cheerfully, because it meant crossing the best game country in the Transvaal. He therefore sent back a message to Paul Kruger to say that we would visit him, and after inspanning our cart we set off for a place called *Olifants Geraamte*, near Rustenburg, at the foot of the Magaliesberg Mountains.

On our journey north to meet Paul Kruger we passed close to the lead mines between Zeerust and Zwartruggens, where we saw a number of Boers quarrying the lead ore. They were melting out the lead and casting it into bullets. In reply to our enquiries as to why they were making so many, they replied, 'We are going to fight the English to get our country back.'

It is impossible to convey any picture of the beauty of the country that we traversed. The veld was fairly alive with game. As far as the eye could see there were blesbok, springbok, wildebeeste, and hartebeeste. The big pans were alive with wild fowl of every description: flamingo, spoonbill, spur-wing geese, Egyptian geese, duck, teal, snipe, and locust

---

1. Conference.
2. Subsequently Paul Kruger became President of the Transvaal Republic.

birds, all in countless numbers, and the veld teemed with korhaan, partridges, *pauw*,[1] and small game.

One afternoon, I remember, we camped on the crest of a hill overlooking a *vlei* about three or four miles in circumference. Whilst the boy was collecting fuel and starting a fire, I went off in search of game. I saw a couple of Egyptian geese on the shore of the *vlei*, and stalked them, killing one and winging the other. The wounded bird swam out into the *vlei*, and I started after him. The water was knee-deep, and I had a wild chase which ended in me killing my goose.

By this time the sun had set. A mile away I could see the camp, with a thread of blue smoke curling up into a blood-red sky. The western heavens looked as if they were on fire—a wonderful mass of molten red reflected on the water. Overhead, at an immense altitude, hung enormous thunderclouds, also mirrored on the still waters of the lake, with incessant lightning playing in their dark depths. All round the shores of the *vlei* countless numbers of antelope of all sorts could be seen, and on the surface of the water and in the air above were hosts of birds, including wild-fowl and crested cranes by the hundred, which circled round uttering their plaintive cry, '*Mooi hem, mooi hem.*' The weird drumming of snipe and the noises made by birds and beasts seemed uncanny to me, standing there alone in the middle of the *vlei*.

Some idea of how tame the game were in those days may be gathered from the fact that I walked up to within fifteen yards of two imperial-crested bustards[2] and shot them both. They weighed 50 lb, and had on them a thick layer of fat like that of a Christmas turkey.

One evening just after we had outspanned, and I was watching the oxen drinking at a small *vlei*, I observed a secretary bird fighting a snake, and was able to pick up a tip worth knowing. I could see that the snake kept striking at the bird's legs and that, every time he struck, the bird dropped his wing like a shield; then, quick as lightning, he kicked the snake before it could recover itself. As the snake showed signs of being played out, the bird stuck its bill into the spine behind the head and killed it.

From this I learned that whenever you have to deal with a bad customer, such as a yellow cobra or rhinkals, the best thing to do is to take off your coat and use it as a shield. I once tried this on with a

---

1. Bustards.

2. *Gom-pauw*.

rhinkals. I had no stick and was trying to kill the snake with a stone. I advanced, holding my coat in front of me, and as the snake spat its venom at me the coat got it all and my eyes were saved.

* * *

On our journey north we passed the large Briton Salt Pan, then owned by the Gous family. At some previous time Kaffirs had evidently been in the habit of stealing salt from this pan, because we saw some skeletons nearby, and it was said that these Kaffirs had been shot for trespassing. The rifle was in those days freely used by the Boer squatters whenever suspicious-looking Kaffirs were found prowling about.

At last we arrived at *Olifants Geraamte*, where we met Paul Kruger and his friends. The party consisted of Dr Jorrison, Piet Joubert, Edward Bok, Paul Kruger and Nicholas Smit, the owner of the farm. They were very glad to see us, as they had been waiting anxiously for Buyskes's arrival.

It did not take long to get down to business, and the whole story of the annexation of the Transvaal by the British was repeated over and over again. Then the petition to Queen Victoria was drafted and redrafted until everyone was satisfied.

Once these discussions had begun they usually lasted till late at night, and I had to wait for the conference to break up before I could make up my bed. Buyskes and I slept in the conference room.

One evening Dr Jorrison asked whether it was wise to discuss secret affairs of state in my presence.

'Oh, he won't repeat anything,' said Paul Kruger. 'He is a young fellow, and some day it will be interesting for him to say he was present on this occasion.'

Then, turning to me, he said, 'Can we trust you?'

Sleepily I replied that I could be trusted not to repeat anything. In reality I was bored with all the talk, and did not for a moment believe in all their heroics.

All the same, I could not help listening to the discussion, and I kept awake because the seats in Nicolaas Smit's house were very hard. I learnt that Smit, Joubert, Jorrison, and Bok had been appointed as a committee for the purpose of obtaining from Great Britain the restoration of the independence of the Transvaal. I did not think it was wrong to listen, because I had given Paul Kruger my word to disclose nothing that I had heard.

Many years later I had the opportunity of reminding Kruger of this meeting. By that time he had become President of the Transvaal, and I had become the head of the firm of H Eckstein, when I was again asked by him not to disclose the nature of a secret document consisting of an acknowledgement of a loan made by my firm to the Transvaal Government on the occasion of the acquisition by the President of certain concessions in Swaziland. These negotiations are described in a subsequent chapter, where I have told how I was able to tell the President that I was the boy who had accompanied Buyskes to *Olifants Geraamte*, and that I had never disclosed to a soul a word of the discussion which I had then overheard.

* * *

After Buyskes had concluded his business with Paul Kruger we proceeded to Pretoria.

Colonel Lanyon had been appointed acting Administrator of the Transvaal, and Sir John Kotze had just become first puisne judge of the Transvaal bench.

I met Sir John at old Mr Juta's house, and told them both all about the bullet-making that I had seen on my journey through the Zeerust district, and how I had heard the Boers say everywhere that they intended to make an attempt to regain their country. Professor Lyall was also present; he had come out from England to advise the Administration on the subject of education.

He turned to me and said, 'Young man, you will find that education alone will overcome the country's difficulties, and when the Dutch people are educated they will realise the necessity for closer union between the two sections of the people.'

On my way back to Kimberley—I think it was at the close of the year 1879—I passed through Potchefstroom. An expedition had just arrived consisting of Dr Wranksley, a naturalist, Dr Sketchly, Dr Crook, and Mr Jamieson, one of the firm of Dublin whisky distillers; he accompanied Stanley, the explorer, a few years later into central Africa, and was a well-known big game hunter. Selous, South Africa's mightiest hunter, was acting as guide to the expedition. They all stayed at the same hotel as that at which I had put up.

I told them also of the significant incident of my coming across a large number of Boers making bullets at the lead mine, and of their talk about fighting to recover their independence.

Upon hearing this, Colonel Tucker of the 80th Regiment, which was stationed at the time in Potchefstroom, exclaimed, 'You need not worry your head about the Boers fighting. I undertake to lead my regiment through South Africa from one end to the other, armed only with pick-handles.'

As a matter of fact, Colonel Tucker received orders the next morning to arrest President Pretorius. Jamieson and Selous offered to go with him, and warned him to beware of falling into a trap. The arrest, however, was made without mishap, but it was one of the causes responsible for the First Boer War.

Two years later, after the defeat of the British forces at Majuba, which was followed by a humiliating peace, I again met Dr Wranksley. He happened to be staying at 'Daddy' Austin's boarding house in Lydenburg in the North-Eastern Transvaal. 'Daddy' was a Cockney, born within the sound of Bow Bells, and there was no mistaking it.

Wranksley put his boots outside his bedroom door to be cleaned, and found them untouched in the morning. The boots were very muddy and dirty, so he called out, 'Hey, boy, come and clean my boots!'

'Daddy' heard this, and came trotting along, saying, 'Clean yer boots! Who the 'ell do you think is going to clean yer boots?'

'All right, guv'nor,' said Wranksley, 'if it is not the custom to clean boots, I suppose I must do without it.'

'Daddy' became interested in his guest, and asked him what his occupation was.

'A naturalist,' replied Wranksley.

'That gets me,' said 'Daddy.'

'Oh, I collect beetles, insects, and such things,' said Wranksley.

'Ah, I know!' said 'Daddy.' 'A butterfly-catcher.'

Wranksley then asked 'Daddy' what his occupation had been before he came to South Africa.

'Daddy' reflected for a moment and said, 'Well, guv'nor, I was a bit of a naturalist myself. I used to catch sparrows, paint 'em, and sell 'em as canaries.'

Chapter 6

I Join Alfred Beit

On my return to Kimberley I started as a diamond broker, and thus I became intimately acquainted with Alfred Beit, then a partner of Jules Porges of Paris, of whose firm Julius Wernher was also a partner. Ultimately, Beit took me into his office in order to train me to become a diamond buyer.

Beit was a native of Hamburg, where he had been born in 1853. His father had given him a very good education, and when he had reached the age of manhood he was apprenticed to the firm of Robinow & Co, who were large diamond-merchants in Amsterdam.

At the age of twenty-two Alfred Beit came to Kimberley, and his previous knowledge of the diamond trade stood him in good stead. He soon became the leading diamond merchant in Kimberley.

One could not help loving the dear man, for he was so perfectly natural and human, and had such a broad outlook on life. He never bore any malice and never said an uncharitable thing about anyone. He had a most unselfish disposition, and was always thoughtful for others. He never forgot a friend.

In business he was a genius, quick to grasp values and take advantage of opportunities. He had such a quick, clear vision that he always saw your point even before you had actually come to it; indeed, he had already made up his mind, often interrupting you halfway through to ask questions.

He was very generous in rewarding anyone who introduced profitable business to him; consequently, most people who had propositions to offer came to him before going to anyone else.

It was a great advantage to a diamond buyer to have the first view of a parcel of diamonds, and we brokers always gave Beit the first chance. Prospectors, also, always went to him first; so did option holders and others.

The combination of Wernher and Beit, when together they founded the well-known firm of Wernher, Beit & Co, which became renowned all over Europe, was very successful, because Beit had all the initiative and creative faculties, whilst Wernher saw to it that all their enterprises were placed on a sound financial basis with adequate reserves. No crisis ever found Wernher unprepared.

If prices slumped and the bottom fell out of the market, Wernher took up all the firm's paper under rebates, and sat ready with a huge cash balance, prepared to take advantage of any business that might be offered to him.

Beit's judgment about markets might sometimes be at fault, leading him at times to make large purchases of shares at a wrong moment, but Wernher would always come to the rescue with the pluck to sell and cut a loss. To my knowledge this happened more than once.

There is no doubt that Beit fell completely under the spell of Cecil Rhodes. Rhodes inspired him with the enthusiasm that urged them both to spend large sums of money in developing the country which subsequently became Rhodesia; and although at that time Germany was looking with envious eyes upon the enormous tract of country over which Rhodes openly declared that the British flag must fly, yet Beit abandoned his German nationality, and became a British subject and an enthusiastic worker for the expansion of the British Empire.

Rhodes had no success with Julius Wernher, although Alfred Beit had little difficulty in persuading Wernher to agree to most of Rhodes's great schemes.

Considering how much Alfred Beit did for South Africa, it is surprising how little is known of the man himself.

Apart from his generous benefactions, which included bequests to the universities of South Africa, he left great sums for railway development in Rhodesia.

ALFRED BEIT

The present generation does not appear to realise, though Beit's contemporaries knew it thirty years ago, that it was largely due to Beit's initiative and support that Rhodes was able to amalgamate the Kimberley diamond mines.

In 1886 it was Beit who helped J B Robinson to form the Robinson Syndicate in order to enable Robinson to buy farms and mines on the Rand.

Beit introduced the Rand gold-mining industry to the share markets of Europe, and attracted capital to South Africa for its development. Under his trusted guidance capital became available for good South African industrial enterprise. Other pioneers followed, but as long as Beit lived, he led the way.

Barney Barnato, in the course of an interview with the late Lord (Nathaniel) Rothschild, was asked what fortunes the various South African magnates had made. When Lord Rothschild asked about Alfred Beit, Barney excitedly replied, 'Ah, Beit! If I had his reputation for honesty, what a fortune I could make!'

Alfred Beit was the best friend South Africa has ever had. He rendered more practical service to the country than any man I know of. He had the kindest, most generous, and loveable nature of any man that ever drew breath.

I give one instance of his generosity; I could give hundreds. I was sorting diamonds in Beit's office in 1880—note the date, for it was before Beit became wealthy. A little girl about twelve years of age came into the office with a note. Beit read it, bit his handkerchief (a favourite habit of his), looked thoughtful for a moment, and then cross-examined the child, asking her the most searching questions. The girl answered them so fearlessly and with such apparent truth, that Beit gave her a note and a cheque for her mother.

I chaffingly asked him if he treated all applicants in the same way, and he tossed the letter over to me. It was from a colonial woman who had lost her husband. She was having a hard time trying to make ends meet and rear a large family. She wrote to the effect that if she could raise enough money to purchase a small shop she could keep afloat. It was characteristic of Beit that he always did the big thing. He had given the little girl £250 to give to her mother.

ALFRED BEIT

And here is another instance of his unselfish, kindly nature. Beit, Hermann Eckstein and I were travelling by coach from Kimberley to Pretoria. Beit had a fox-terrier puppy that he was taking up for one of my sisters. About twenty miles from Pretoria we were bowling along on a good hard road in bright moonlight at about 2 am when suddenly the axle snapped and over went the coach. The forepart of it came away, and the horses galloped off with it. I happened to be on the top side and managed to get out of the window first. I glanced round to see what had happened, and saw the driver lying stunned by the roadside. Nothing stirred. I called out to Beit and Eckstein, asking if they were hurt. The only answer I got was, 'Where is Jackie (the pup)?'

One by one I helped the passengers out of the coach till only Beit remained. Everyone had trodden on him trying to get out, but in his search for Jackie he had felt nothing.

In the upset everything was topsy-turvy, so that when we finally found Jackie he was underneath a pile of rugs and cushions fast asleep. Having satisfied himself that Jackie was unhurt, Beit at once went round to see if any of the passengers had received any injury. The driver by this time had recovered. It was Beit who accompanied me on a six mile walk to get assistance at a neighbouring farm.

* * *

Early in 1880 my brother Bill wanted to go to England to establish an agency there, and Beit agreed that I should look after my brother's interests on a profit-sharing basis. We did an enormous business, and very soon acquired a considerable fortune.

For some time I had been longing to visit England. I therefore took advantage of a lull in the market to pay my first visit to the home of my forebears. I sailed from Cape Town in the Union Company's steamship *Trojan*, under the command of Captain Coxwell, in October 1881, and landed in England in a snowstorm. Most of my fellow passengers were British officers, returning from the war in the Transvaal, which was entirely an Imperial affair. Many of them were beardless lieutenants, who in later years became well-known generals.

I spent a few months with my brother, who had already been in England for some time, and later on I toured the Continent with my friend, J C Rimer, visiting the capitals of most of the European countries.

JULES PORGES

Chapter 7

Pilgrim's Rest

I returned to Kimberley in 1882 and found that the bottom had fallen out of the market. Everything had gone wrong in my absence. I had lost heavily, and I could see that I would be obliged to make a fresh start. Just at that time reports of rich gold discoveries in the North-Eastern Transvaal filtered through to Kimberley, and I decided to go up and try my luck there.

I went by coach to Pretoria, which was then quite a small village with pretty rose hedges growing round the gardens of the houses. There I bought a cart and four oxen from a man who went by the name of 'Yankee Wilson.' Over the cart was a canvas tent, on which was stencilled a large American eagle. When I had stowed away all my belongings I picked up a Shangaan native, who rejoiced in the name of 'Shilling,' and was on his way to Kimberley to work in the mines. I managed to persuade him to change his mind and come with me, and we started off for Lydenberg.

Pilgrim's Rest in the Lydenburg district had been and still was a busy gold-mining centre in the early 'eighties. Alluvial gold had been found in the creeks, and men had come from all parts of the world to try their luck. Fairly large nuggets had been found, and up to the date of my visit I was told that about a million pounds had been won.

THE AUTHOR'S BROTHER,∆ WP TAYLOR

Having passed through Pilgrim's Rest, I came to Mac Mac, so named by the natives because most of the diggers working there were Scotsmen with names beginning with Mac. There I found Bob Jameson, a brother of Dr Jameson, who, in 1895, was destined to become the leader of the Jameson Raid.

Bob was a mining man who had gained considerable experience in gold mining in Australia. He represented the Kimberley Syndicate that owned the Mac Mac property, which had been acquired from Tom McLaughlan (a friend of M'bandini, the Swazi king). Bob was living in Tom McLaughlan's old house when I arrived, and here we were joined by Dr Jameson, Dr Hans Sauer, and Dr Oscar Summershield. We spent a very happy time together. We passed most of our evenings playing cards, and on one occasion we played a game of freeze-out poker. It did not take long for Dr Jameson to freeze out Dr Summershield and me. Dr Hans Sauer had more assets than we had, and fought on; but he eventually succumbed, having lost everything, even his top boots.

* * *

At that time a man by the name of David Benjamin had obtained from the Government a concession to mine reefs near the Blyde River, and what was named the Morgenzon concession had been granted to three Dutchmen, Schalk Burger (afterwards Vice-President of the Transvaal), Diedrich Muller, and Abel Erasmus, who was Native Commissioner. During the British occupation, Abel Erasmus was the man who had been accused by General Sir Garnet Wolseley of stirring up the Kaffir Chief, Mapoch, to rebel against the Government, and it is said that a reward of £500 had been offered for his capture. Mrs Abel Erasmus hated the Kaffirs, and insisted on her husband carrying out his duties with the greatest severity. If he happened to be away, she would mete out punishment to any delinquent Kaffir with her own hand. The Kaffirs hated her, and when she eventually became blind they put her affliction down to the power of their witchdoctors. Muller was a farmer and brother-in-law of Erasmus.

Hearing that these three men had acquired this concession, I proceeded to Kruger's Post to interview them. They proposed to me that I should join them, and we soon came to an agreement that I should find

THIS CONTEMPORARY DRAWING ILLUSTRATES THE SORT OF ROADS OVER WHICH PIONEERS HAD TO TRAVEL

the money for working their proposition while they were to draw their shares of the profits.

I had heard that Arthur Neale, my old Kimberley friend, was mining in the Ross Hill district, and I was very anxious to see him. To get to his camp I had to travel by a road which was very bad and even dangerous, but my tented cart was very comfortable even though its progress was slow. Frequently when the track was very steep I had to take the wheels off and slide the body of the cart down with *riems*,[1] held back by a gang of Kaffirs. In spite of flooded rivers and many narrow escapes, we managed to pull through.

I do not know what the tracks are like now, but in 1883 we old pioneers thought it was a pretty tough proposition to negotiate the road between Lydenburg and Spitzkop with an ox-wagon or cart.

I must admit that I was terrified as I looked down far below me at the remains of broken wagons that had fallen down the precipitous slopes through the carelessness of their unskilled drivers. I had heard of the evil reputation borne by the Devil's Knuckles over which I had to pass, and concluded that it was well named.

I shall never forget the view from the top of the mountain before taking the steep descent to Ross Hill. It was truly magnificent. Standing as I was in the full blaze of the rising sun, I gazed over the low country covered with a white cloth of mist, or shall we say a sea of snow, through which the peaks of Spitzkop and other hills were peeping, their heads tinted with pink by the rays the rising sun. Looking over the mist, I could see the Lebombo range in the far distance to the east. Turning to the south, I could clearly see the Barberton Mountains and to the north of me the Lulu peaks were plainly visible. As my eyes searched the horizon eerie sounds came drifting up through the fog. I could just distinguish baboons sunning themselves on the rocky ledges below me, and here and there a *klipspringer* would suddenly come into view and as quickly drop out of sight. As the sun rose higher the birds began to wake, and their song, mingled with the *Chi-chilluh* call of the red-winged partridge, was to be heard on every side.

Time was pressing, and I was thankful to arrive at last at Neale's camp in time for breakfast. His camp was at Ross Hill near Spitzkop,

---

1. Rawhide ropes.

whose peak travellers to the Game Reserve[1] today can see pointing upwards through the clouds.

I spent several days with Neale looking at the alluvial washing that was being carried on close by. I told him that I was going to work the Morgenzon Concession, and asked him to join me. To this he agreed, and the next morning we started off together to Pilgrim's.

On nearing Mac Mac, Neale thought there was a chance of shooting a duck. Taking his gun and a canvas haversack he strolled off to a small sheet of water that we could see in the distance. After an hour had passed he arrived back with a duck in the haversack. I looked inside and found that the bird was still alive. I therefore took it out, knocked its head on a stone, and replaced it in the bag.

As we neared Mac Mac, we could see Tom McLaughlan's house in the distance, and next to it were a few huts owned by a man whose Kaffir name was *Mattit man*. He kept a tiny store, and as we wanted some mealie meal I gave my 'boy' Shilling half a sovereign and told him to go and buy a bucketful of meal while we outspanned and prepared a fire.

Investigation of our larder showed us that the duck and the mealie meal were going to constitute all we were going to have for supper. I opened the game bag and threw the duck out for the 'boy' to clean. With a flapping of wings and a parting 'Quack, quack!' the duck flew off and, when two hundred yards from the camp, it towered to a considerable height and then fell in a thick patch of tambooki grass.

To see our supper fly off just as we were about to cook it was more than we could stand, but hope revived when we saw the bird tower and fall. We marked the spot with great care, collected a few friendly Kaffirs, and commenced to search.

How we searched! The Kaffirs, convinced that the bird was *tagati*,[2] soon melted away, but Neale and I had to find our supper; so we stuck to it, and finally found the duck cold and stiff, but to make doubly sure this time we cut its head off. We admitted to each other that our anxiety passed off only when the bird was boiling in the pot.

Meantime, Shilling had returned with a bucket of mealie meal, but no change.

---

1. This is probably a reference to the Kruger National Park — Ed.
2. Bewitched.

The price of mealie meal was 7s 6d per 200 lb. Clearly there was some mistake, so off we started to the store to investigate the matter. The store was a flimsy affair of mud and grass, with a few gin cases as a counter. Behind this stood a typical *rooinek*—a youth of about twenty—red-haired, burnt, blistered, and freckled by the sun, eyes that twinkled with merriment, and a smile that completely captivated us. All our hostility vanished. Mildly we enquired whether the 'boy' had been given any change, because ten shillings was far too much for a bucket of meal.

With a disarming smile, the young man handed me back my half-sovereign.

'I'm sorry,' he said, 'I'm a newcomer, a stranger in the land, and I had no idea what I ought to charge you. Would you mind settling with the owner of the store the next time you may be passing?'

'All right,' I said, 'what is your name and where do you hail from?'

'Percy Fitzpatrick, from the Cape,' was the reply.

This was my first meeting with my life-long friend, who afterwards became Sir Percy Fitzpatrick.

* * *

From Mac Mac, Neale and I had an adventurous journey, having to cross the Blyde River many times before reaching Pilgrim's Rest. However, we arrived at last and, after laying in a supply of stores, we made camp on Pilgrim's Hill, building ourselves a wattle and daub house.

After working at Morgenzon for some time, the Williams family joined us. They had originally come from Bloemfontein. There were three brothers, of whom the eldest, 'Tempe,' was married to one of President Steyn's sisters. I had met the Williams family before when I was trying my luck washing alluvial gravel on Pilgrim's Creek, soon after I arrived in the Lydenburg district, and it was from them that I had learned that the Morgenzon concession could be acquired.

* * *

While Neale and I were working at Morgenzon, Gardener Williams, who subsequently became general manager of the De Beers Company, was general manager of the Transvaal Gold Mining and Exploration Company at Pilgrim's Rest. He was a well-known mining engineer, and enjoyed the full confidence of the Rothschilds.

Gardener Williams took a kindly interest in the work I was doing at Morgenzon and was good enough to arrange for me to learn mine sampling, and also amalgamation of gold on copper plates. Thanks to the practical teaching I received, I became a competent mine sampler.

* * *

The healthy, open-air life that we led on the slopes of the Pilgrim's Rest mountain was very attractive. The climate of that district is, perhaps, the finest in South Africa, for the air comes off the Indian Ocean and brings with it a mist very similar to what one experiences in Scotland. These mists can be very dense on the mountaintops, and care must be taken not to be caught in one when out shooting or prospecting.

The value of the land in the Pilgrim's Rest area is being appreciated today by the land companies which own most of it, and tree planting on a very extensive scale is being carried out. The riverbeds are also being rewashed for alluvial gold. The scenery is remarkably fine, particularly about Mac Mac. Mount Anderson is about 8 000 feet above sea level. It is a magnificent mountain, once densely occupied by a people who terraced its slopes. There are numerous waterfalls and wooded ravines, yielding a great variety of verdure and flora. Tree ferns are everywhere to be seen growing luxuriantly.

I used to walk all over the hills, and sometimes even as far as Lydenburg and back in two days, spending the night dancing. It was a pretty strenuous trip as the distance each way was about thirty-six miles.

I used to see a lot of Edward Chester and Charlie Hancock, both of whom were mining in the district. I remember that, on the occasion of one of our visits to Lydenburg, we were hailed by Miss Cubitt, who later became Lady Fitzpatrick.

She called to us from her window, 'Have you come in for the dance?'

As a matter of fact we had not known that there was to be a dance on that night. Anyhow, we stayed for it and danced till dawn, when we set out on our return journey and reached the mine somewhat late for the day's work.

Chapter 8

Gold Mining in the Early 'Eighties

Many people are still alive who remember Ike Sonnenberg in the early days of Kimberley and the Lydenburg diggings. He furnished South Africa with many amusing stories. Ike was a professional gambler, and although I have heard many stories of Ike's slickness, I can positively say from my personal experience, which extended over many years, that Ike was an honest player and totally unable to fake cards. He was, however, a match for anyone who tried to cheat him.

On one occasion, Ike found himself in a bar at Moodies and was asked to play cards by notorious cardsharpers. Ike made some excuse, but the two sharpers persisted to such an extent that he finally said he would play, only on condition, however, that the barman shuffled and dealt the cards.

This brought down so much chaff on the heads of the two sharpers that Ike was able to escape.

Ike and I once travelled in the old post-cart from Lydenburg to Pretoria. I was on one of my periodical visits to my family, who had settled down there. It was a bright, frosty, moonlit night, and bitterly cold. We were seated on the top of the mailbags holding on to the ropes that fastened them down. At about 2 am, as we were passing through the

Crocodile Valley and were nearing the station for the next change of horses, we passed a farm belonging to Christian Joubert, who hated the English very cordially, and at that early hour it seemed hopeless to wake up the old Boer for a cup of coffee. However, Ike was determined to try.

Turning to me, he said, 'What will you give for a cup of coffee?'

'A sovereign,' I replied.

'Done,' said Ike. 'Come with me.'

The pair of us, shivering with cold, rapped at the door, and a gruff voice from within asked what we wanted.

'It's me, Mr Joubert, my name is Sonnenberg. I come from Lydenburg by the post-cart. My wife told me not to pass your place without paying for the vegetables she bought from Mrs Joubert and, being an honourable man, I wish to pay the debt. Will you please open the door, and let me pay you?' (Of course, Ike had made this story up.)

We heard mutterings and Mrs Joubert's voice saying, 'Christian, go and fetch the money.' Presently the top half of the door was slightly opened and a bleary-eyed, white-bearded old gentleman, holding a candle, put out his hand for the money, into which Ike slipped a sovereign. Old Christian protested he had no change. I therefore slipped my hand down, unfastened the lever of the lower door, and pushed it open.

We both walked in. 'Oh, never mind the change,' said Ike. 'Give us two cups of coffee and call it quits.'

Old Christian started to protest, and offered to return the money, but the old lady had overheard the conversation from her warm bed. She called out, 'Tell the girl to light the fire and give them coffee.' Ike had won. It was worth it.

* * *

It was customary in the old Republic days of the Transvaal for President Kruger to tour the country between the sessions of the *Volksraad*.[1]

While I was mining at Pilgrim's Rest, I happened to visit Lydenburg on the day that *Oom* Paul was holding a meeting. I saw a big crowd in the marketplace, and got as close as I could to the platform.

---

1. Transvaal Parliament.

The President had recently returned from Europe, where he had been trying to get the suzerainty clause of his treaty with England withdrawn. He was telling his audience all he had seen in England, and was just then describing the British Mint, how sovereigns were made, the accuracy of the weighing machines, and the instrument like an elephant's trunk that seized any coin that was below the correct weight and rejected it.

The audience listened in an amused way, but I could see that they were becoming bored with Kruger's stories. They had come to the meeting with grievances and wanted them ventilated. Frequent whisperings and nudgings told me that somebody was going to bait the President.

I did not have to wait long. A Boer among the crowd shouted that they had heard enough about Europe and its wonders. What they wanted to know was where the Lydenburg farmers were going to find a market for their produce. During the British occupation, they said, they had always had a good market, and mealies then fetched 15s to 20s a bag. The Boer wound up by saying, '*Waar is de verdomde Engelsman nouw*?'[1]

Kruger was not long in taking up the challenge. He began by asking the farmer who had spoken how many bags of mealies he produced a year.

The Boer answered, 'About three hundred.'

'How many bags do you require for your own purposes?'

'About one hundred and fifty,' was the answer.

'There,' said the President, 'that is what I always find when I am asked these questions. Here is a farmer who only needs one hundred and fifty bags of mealies a year, and he goes to the trouble of producing three hundred! I have no patience with such people.'

Evidently he thought he had scored off his questioner, because they all cried, '*Hoor, hoor*!'[2]

* * *

1. 'Where is the damned Englishman now?' — Ed.
2. 'Hear, hear!' — Ed.

Good shooting was to be had in the winter months along the banks of the Sabie River and its tributaries. There was an abundance of game, wood and water were plentiful, and camping was a joy.

On one occasion our party consisted, beside myself, of Teddy Blacklaw, George Roy and Charlie Holland. We were enjoying excellent sport, and had returned to camp a little before sunset. The rifles had been stacked against a tree, and the party was busy washing and preparing for the evening meal when the Kaffirs called out, '*M'ditcha*! *M'ditcha*!'[1]

Sure enough, one hundred yards away in an open glade, we saw two wild dogs leaping in the air. Evidently they had 'run cunning,' and were looking for their quarry.

In various stages of undress, we all ran for our rifles—which we had barely seized when an impala doe came into view, pursued by more wild dogs. The two wild dogs we had first seen cut in and bowled the impala over. Four shots rang out before the dogs could seize their prey.

The dogs sheered off into the bush, and we ran to rescue the doe. We found her quite exhausted and breathing heavily. We then sent the 'boys' for water, which we poured over her, forcing some into her mouth and fanning her. In a little while she began to recover, and tried to rise. We administered another douche, and then left her alone, watching to see what she would do.

Presently she got up and looked round in a bewildered sort of way. Then she trotted up to us, as if for further protection, turned, and looked in every direction to see if there were any more enemies still about. Apparently assured that we had driven them off, she gave us a long, grateful look of thanks, and disappeared into the bush.

The wild dogs had gone off in the opposite direction. We found blood tracks, but it was too late to follow them up.

Those who have read Sir Percy Fitzpatrick's book, *Jock of the Bushveld*, will remember this story, which I told him. When it appeared in his book, he wrote me a letter—which is mentioned later—acknowledging the source of the story.

Fitz, as we used to call him, frequently visited our camp in those days, and while he was with us I had the misfortune to lose a pointer dog of which I was very fond. After we had given the dog a decent burial, Fitz pinned the following lines on the grave:

---

1. 'Wild dog, wild dog!'

'Here lies poor Jack, whose flame of life
In early youth was snuffed.
He never failed to score a "point,"
A chance he never muffed.

True and steady was poor Jack,
No fault, no foible even.
One "point," alas, too much he made;
'Twas when he "stood" on Heaven.'

* * *

The doings of our neighbours in the district were of great interest to us, and sometimes afforded us plenty of excitement. The Transvaal Gold and Land Company, under the management of Gardner Williams, was mining on Brown's Hill. At Graskop many diggers were sluicing for gold, and the Lisbon-Berlin Gold Mines had commenced operations on the eastern side of Pilgrim's Rest.

The latter company had been formed in London by Baron Grant, the donor of Leicester Square and the man who obtained the first concession for building the Delagoa Bay Railway.

Everything was being done on the Lisbon-Berlin property on a grand scale. Hydraulic machinery, stamp batteries, and other mining-machinery, together with a staff of American experts, arrived on the ground long before payable gold had been discovered.

After a time disputes arose between the employees and the manager, and those who had not received their pay threw up their jobs.

I happened to be in Lydenburg the night that McLellan, the Company's manager, shot Hobbs, the Company's geologist. We had all dined together, and when dinner was over McLellan and Hobbs strolled off together across the market-square towards Stafford Parker's bar, where card-playing with Ike Sonnenberg and others was usually carried on until the small hours.

Crossing the square to the bar, Hobbs and McLellan had a dispute, and Hobbs drew his gun. McLellan made an effort to seize it, and in the struggle that followed the gun exploded and Hobbs was killed. This naturally caused great excitement in the district. McLellan gave himself up and was tried for murder, but after a short trial he was acquitted. At the trial public sympathy was certainly on the side of the accused, because Hobbs had been the aggressor.

One of the engineers sent out by the Lisbon-Berlin Company to erect machinery on its property was an American named Judd Coppach. The Company had failed to pay Judd his wages, and the sum that had accumulated to his credit had become quite large. Judd therefore decided to go to London and interview Baron Grant, the Chairman of the Company.

Judd called twice at the Baron's office, and each time was informed that the Baron was out. The third time he called he told the clerk that he would await the Baron's return and, after settling himself down in a chair in the waiting-room, he took a Colt revolver out of his pocket and laid it on the table in front of him.

It happened that the London office had heard of the McLellan-Hobbs episode, and when the clerk, who was aware of the fact that the Baron was all the time in his office, realised that he had to deal with a desperado, he took fright and went and told the Baron what had happened. Back came the clerk with a message to say, 'Would Mr Coppach please state the nature of his business in writing.'

Judd thereupon asked for paper, pen, and ink, and this is what he wrote:

> 'To Baron Grant, your Lord Almightyness. It is beneath the dignity of an American citizen to call three times for his money. I have done so, and unless I get a cheque at once it would have been better if your mother had been "barren".'

Judd got his money.

* * *

In the year 1883 there was a good deal of talk of the gold discoveries at Moodies in the Barberton district. Some years previously George Piggott-Moodie had received from the Transvaal Republican Government a large farm in the Kaap Valley in payment for some survey work that he had done in defining the Swaziland boundary. On this farm gold had been found by a prospector called 'French Bob,' who named his discovery 'The Pioneer Reef.' A number of people had come up from

Natal and elsewhere; some of them formed a syndicate to work the Ivy Reef and various small propositions in the neighbourhood.

I therefore left Neale in charge at Morgenzon and set out on horseback for Barberton, where I found that I was among the first arrivals on the scene of the discovery. I visited a good many small properties on which gold reefs had been opened up, and I stayed with Willie Anderson, at that time Moodie's general manager. I was not particularly impressed by what I saw, and after a fairly thorough investigation I returned to Morgenzon.

However, I had not been back very long before rumours drifted in from Barberton to the effect that Edwin Bray had 'struck it very rich' in a mine that he had named the 'Sheba.' This made me decide that there would probably be far greater opportunities and far more activity in Barberton than I had at first anticipated.

I heard that Barber and Rimer had erected a battery near the present site of Barberton, which was the name they gave to the small township they laid out.

I therefore again set off for Barberton, leaving Neale once more in charge of the Morgenzon concession. As we were not making it pay, owing to the many difficulties with which we had to contend, I realised that I could not expect Neale to stay on. When he finally left the district, I heard that he married a relation of Steyn, President of the Orange Free State, and the concession reverted to the owners and subsequently became the Clewer Mine.

I travelled all the way to Barberton *via* Lydenburg and the Duiwel's Kantoor in my old scotch-cart drawn by my four oxen, driven by my boy, Shilling. I had to follow the old hunters' wheel-tracks, for there were no roads. I frequently had to resort to my old practice of taking the wheels off the cart and sliding the body down the steep mountainside. At Elands River we were nearly washed away in the flooded river, but I had to run risks because I wanted to be among the first at the new goldfield.

An Italian by the name of Marinni, who was a very fine piccolo player, followed me in a wagon. To my horror, I saw him being washed away in the swollen river. I managed to pull him out, but he lost his wagon.

On my way to Barberton, I camped one night in my cart in a little hollow on the slopes of the Duiwel's Kantoor mountain. It was a very attractive spot surrounded by a bewildering mass of rock, bush, and wild vegetation. A stream of crystal clear water flowed down a creek. It was an ideal spot for a camp.

That night a storm broke with unusual severity, and the incessant lightning ran along the boulder-capped ridges around me in an awesome manner. It was so terrifying that for the twenty minutes during which it lasted I almost gave up hope of coming through alive. When the next day I told the folk at Barretts where I had spent the previous night, they told me that it was the worst place for lightning in that district, because of the quantity of magnetic ironstone that outcropped in the valley. I must confess that all through that night I was wondering what was going to happen to me while the lightning was so fierce, because I was sleeping on a wire mattress that I had fixed on the bottom of my cart.

On my journey one night I had made my camp, and after I had finished my supper I was soon fast asleep. I had tied my oxen up to the trek-chain a little distance away from the cart, because the insects worried the cattle and made them so restless that they kept me awake. It was a lovely, clear, moonlit night.

Soon after midnight I awoke with the feeling that something was wrong, and called out to Shilling, asking whether the cattle were all right. He sleepily called back, 'Yes,' but I had a pre-sentiment that all was not well, and got up to investigate. The oxen had disappeared.

I quickly pulled on my boots and, grabbing my rifle, I jumped out of the cart and climbed a little rise. There I could just make out my oxen being driven off by two men. I promptly opened fire on the two thieves, but the light was too bad for accurate shooting. However, I had evidently scared them to death, for they ran for their lives, and I got my cattle back.

* * *

I soon settled down at Barberton, opened an office, and began business as a sharebroker. Here I met Edouard Lippert, Alfred Beit's cousin. He was a short, round-shouldered man with very pronounced Hebraic features, and a sandy beard. He was very musical, and he spoke perfect English with a great charm of manner. He was well read and extremely clever, and he was one of the ablest men in South Africa. He was not very popular, but his enemies feared him. He was married, but had no family. His wife was a very dear lady, and commanded universal respect. In appearance she was very plain, but her charm, her beautiful character, and her many accomplishments made her beloved by everyone.

Lippert and I agreed to lease a large bungalow on what was called the Berea. We kept house together, and one of my sisters joined us. Thus we lived happily enough until one day Edouard Lippert and I had a difference of opinion over a commission of £250, which I claimed was mine. It was a case of not having everything in writing when dealing with a shifty customer. This was the beginning of a breach between us.

* * *

Barberton was not then connected by telegraph with the outside world until some time after my arrival and, as I was doing a considerable business with my Kimberley clients, I had to send my telegraphic messages from Middelburg. For this purpose I employed Harry Pitt, a brother of Mrs Hermann Eckstein, to take my telegrams on horseback between Barberton and Middelburg, a distance of about 136 miles. The messages were in code, and in order that I might not excite too much curiosity, I used to take my dog and gun and ride out to meet Pitt soon after I supposed he had left Middelburg.

As I had my codebook in my saddlebag, I was therefore able to choose some quiet, shady spot, and decode the telegrams that he brought me, after which he would start back to Middelburg with fresh telegrams.

By this means I could maintain a rapid telegraphic service with Kimberley. Moreover, as I always took my gun with me, and generally brought back a bird or two that I had managed to shoot, my coming and going excited no gossip.

I also corresponded regularly by letter with Alfred Beit, who was still in Kimberley, and I did a considerable business during the boom by sending my clients' shares in new companies for sale on consignment to Alfred Beit, who passed them on to Leopold Hirsh in London, where they were sold. Hirsh had previously done a big business for Alfred Beit in the disposal of diamond shares.

I soon became a director of many companies, including the Sheba Mine, whose £1 shares rose to £40 and over.

PROMINENT MEN IN THE BUSINESS AND SOCIAL LIFE
OF KIMBERLEY IN 1886
Back row: J Caldicott, Max Michaelis, Dr Rutherford-Harris
Sir Charles Metcalfe, Henry Robinow
Front row: Richard Solomon, Mr Justice Searle, Dr Jameson, JB Taylor,
William Solomon, J Kilgour

I also examined many of the Barberton mines very carefully, and eventually came to the conclusion that in the long run they would turn out to be unpayable. I therefore strongly advised Beit to sell out all his Barberton interests. I made up my mind that, except for the Oriental and the Sheba Mine, there were no properties likely to come up to expectations.

Beit was reluctant to follow my advice without the confirmation of another opinion. He therefore lost no time in requisitioning the services of both Gardner Williams and J S Curtis, instructing them to proceed to Barberton and make a thorough investigation of the prospects of payable gold-mining shares.

On their arrival they came to stay with me, and visited many mines. I had told them beforehand my opinion, and I was pleased to find that when they had completed their investigations they were able to tell me that they agreed that Beit would be well advised to have nothing further to do with Barberton.

As soon as Beit received their report he decided to visit Barberton and look round for himself. He brought with him Jules Porges and Sigismund Neumann,[1] a Kimberley diamond-buyer.

Previous to his arrival in Barberton, Beit had taken part in the formation of the Robinson Syndicate for the purpose of purchasing farms and claims on the new goldfields on the Rand. In their journey over the Witwatersrand they had visited these properties. On their arrival at Barberton I met them and put them up at my house.

Beit's energy when inspecting shafts and drives was really astonishing. From early dawn until dark he would ride and walk over the roughest country without showing signs of fatigue. On most of these expeditions we took Percy Fitzpatrick with us. He kept us amused, as he was always very good company. Porges sometimes came too, and once we persuaded Neumann to join us.

We travelled on horseback, lived on sardines and biscuits, and slept in any hut that we happened to strike at about sunset. Fitz and I used to take a keen delight in telling snake stories, and we soon had Neumann's nerves on edge.

One evening we reached 'French Bob's' camp, which consisted of a grass hut about 12 feet by 15 feet. In one corner French Bob had a bed

---

1. Subsequently created a baronet.

made of poles and sacking raised a few feet off the ground. Beit's shakedown was almost under French Bob's bed. The rest of us lay in rows on a bed of bracken, with coats and blankets thrown over it. Of course, we slept in our clothes. Fitz and I had Neumann between us. Somehow a sjambok had been left on the floor in the making up of the beds, and we soon discovered that it was lying under Neumann with one end projecting on Fitz's side and the other end sticking out near me. By carefully moving the sjambok backwards and forwards we gave Neumann the feeling that he had something alive under his back. At the same time we told him about the deadly bite of the mamba and other venomous snakes. Neumann nearly died of fright, and it took us some time to persuade him that his snake was only a sjambok.

Chapter 9

The Rand

So many extraordinary statements have been published regarding the first mining operations on the Rand that it is as well, for historical accuracy, that facts should be stated.

In 1883 the Strubens found traces of gold in creeks and also in reefs in the Witwatersrand area, and in 1884 the elder brother, Henry Struben, purchased two small farms to the north-west of the Witwatersrand, where both the brothers continued to prospect energetically. In the summer of 1884, a gold-bearing reef was discovered and traced by Fred Struben for several miles. Rich pockets were found which assayed several ounces of gold and silver to the ton. This rich occurrence, situated about fifteen miles from the present site of Johannesburg, was considered to be of primary importance, and the Strubens erected a five-stamp mill. They succeeded, however, in recovering only about 8 dwts of gold to the ton.

It was in the same year that prospecting for gold became active in the Pretoria and Heidelberg districts. In fact, prospecting was carried on over a wide area, and was stimulated not only by the reports published by the Strubens that they had found payable gold on their farm, but also by the fact that they had crushed a considerable quantity of ore. The gold recovered by Harry Struben was exhibited by him in Pretoria, and caused quite a sensation.

Experienced miners, however, examined the property and came to the conclusion that the Strubens were too optimistic. They expressed the opinion that although gold had been found, it did not exist in payable quantities.

As work proceeded on the reef which had been christened 'The Confidence Reef,' the results became very disappointing, for it was soon proved that the gold existed only in a small deposit. The Strubens had spent several thousands on their mining operations. However, the fact that gold was being found had a very stimulating effect, and this led to active prospecting on the outcrops of the conglomerate reefs which abounded on the Witwatersrand.

There was no question of these conglomerate reefs having to be *discovered*, because they outcropped three or four feet, and could be followed for miles as they stretched away both to the east and to the west.

* * *

My family was living in Pretoria at the time, and on the occasion of one of my visits to them I met Harry Struben, who told me that he and his brother Fred were still working on their farm *Kromdraai*, to the north of the Witwatersrand. He invited me to go and see his mine, which I did; but I was not very much impressed.

Fred Struben, to whom undoubtedly should be given the honour of having called the world's attention to the existence and payability of the Rand conglomerate rock, was absent from the farm looking for something better, and was actively prospecting and sampling every outcrop that appeared to be promising.

I saw Harry Struben again shortly afterwards, and he told me that a man called George Walker, one of his brother's employees, assisted by an Australian by the name of Harrison, had discovered on the farm *Langlaagte* a rich reef, which afterwards became known as the Main Reef Leader.

Both George Honeyball and J G Bantjes can also enjoy the honour of having been among those who were the first prospectors to point out the continuity of the Witwatersrand conglomerate outcrops.

Even I might have ranked as one of the first discoverers, as the following episode will reveal.

While I was still at Barberton, and long before I had made up my mind to take up my residence on the Witwatersrand, I was invited to shoot over Sammy Marks's farm on the Vaal River, where the town of Vereeniging now stands. I therefore went by coach from Barberton to Pretoria, where I joined our shooting party of five, consisting of 'Long Piet' Marais, Arty Walker, George Hudson, the British Resident, and my brother Bill.

We travelled from Pretoria by ox-wagon and crossed the Orange Grove Hills. The road was very rocky, and we had some trouble in getting through. It was here that I shot a tufted partridge, the only specimen that I have ever seen in South Africa.

On nearing the farm *Langlaagte* on the Witwatersrand, on which one of the richest mines in the world, called the Robinson Mine, was afterwards established, we were threatened by a heavy thunderstorm and decided to outspan near some water. For miles there was no sign of any habitation.

When we had made camp, my brother and I took one of our Kaffir 'boys' down to the *spruit* to get some water. There was a *vlei* close by, and we thought that there might be a chance of shooting a few snipe for supper. We walked along the outcrop of a reef running east and west, which stood up like shark-fins in places, two or three feet above the surface of the veld. It was a conglomerate reef, containing large pebbles, many of which were easily detached, although they were mostly embedded in the quartzite rock. The conglomerate nature of the reefs struck us as being very unusual, but they appeared to me to be worth sampling for gold. We therefore knocked off three or four chunks with a view to crushing and panning them on our return to Pretoria.

I must confess that my brother was much keener than I was, because I had never heard of gold being found in conglomerate rock. Anyhow, we threw the samples of reef into a sack and the next morning left for Vereeniging, about thirty miles to the south.

JB ROBINSON

It was only when we eventually returned to Pretoria that I found that our Kaffir 'boy' had been using our rock samples to support his pots and kettles over the open fire on which he cooked our meals, and had left them behind.

I had to go back to Barberton, but my brother, who was living in Pretoria at the time and prospecting for minerals, promised that he would take the first opportunity of collecting more samples from the same reef as soon as he returned to the neighbourhood. This he never did, and nothing much was heard of the reef until 1886, although there were many wagon-tracks crossing the outcrop that must have been known to hundreds of travellers. In telling this story I merely wish to record that only an unfortunate accident deprived me of the privilege of ranking as at least one of the discoverers of the Rand.

* * *

When I reported to my brother what Struben had told me of the new discoveries on the farm *Langlaagte*, he immediately went over to the Witwatersrand to examine the reef that had been exposed by cross-trenching. I asked him to take samples and send them to Alfred Beit. This he did. At the same time many prospectors, such as Henry Norse, Bantjes, and others, working for various syndicates, were digging trenches across the reef and sinking holes. Some of them made good discoveries; for instance, Japie De Villiers's Syndicate struck it very rich, and in July of the year 1886 specimens of the ore found by him were also sent to Kimberley.

The showing was so remarkable that J B Robinson, backed by Alfred Beit, who had seen the pannings, left for the Rand on the following day with instructions to acquire mining interests in the name of a syndicate to be called the Robinson Syndicate. The Kimberley to Pretoria coach-road ran through Potchefstroom and thence north-east to Pretoria, leaving the little pioneer town, then called 'Ferreira Camp,' now part of Johannesburg, some fifteen or twenty miles to the east. But Robinson drove straight to the little mining camp.

Among the first to arrive on the Rand from Kimberley with J B Robinson was Dr Hans Sauer, who secured options to purchase several properties in the hope that Rhodes would take them up. His hopes were doomed to disappointment, because when Rhodes arrived on the Rand he refused to follow Sauer's advice.

Among those who had commenced working on the reef, besides De Villiers, were Colonel Ferreira, Henry Nourse, Bantjes, Walker, and many others. Here also Fred Struben was particularly active. He lost no time in putting down a small shaft on that part of the reef on which the Crown Mines is now situated. He mined about fifty tons of gold-bearing ore and carted them over to his battery at *Kromdraai*. So satisfied was he at the result that he applied for *mynpacht* rights.

The *Volksraad* had passed the Gold Law, which recognised the right of the owner of land to select his *mynpacht*; in other words, the section which he intended to use for his own mining operations. Struben applied for a *mynpacht* and was granted the first of these rights given out to anyone on the Rand. This *mynpacht* ultimately became the Crown Reef Mine, then under lease, the reversion rights belonging to the owners of *Langlaagte*.

In granting the *mynpacht* to Struben, the *Volksraad*, in August of the same year (1886), passed a vote of thanks to him as the discoverer of payable gold on the Rand.

* * *

In the meanwhile J B Robinson was operating on behalf of the Robinson Syndicate, the members of which were Alfred Beit, J B Robinson, and Marcus, who was Robinson's partner. The capital of this syndicate was £30 000. With this backing, Robinson lost no time in buying up farms on which the existence of the reef had been established and where the presence of payable gold had been proved.

As soon as Robinson reported what he had done, Beit cabled the information to his senior partner, Jules Porges. Jules Porges of Paris, Julius Wernher of London, and Alfred Beit of Kimberley were then closely associated in partnership. Thus was the money found for Robinson's purchases, and with Beit behind him Robinson certainly had the courage of his opinions. He spent money lavishly, and Beit always supported him. Although Robinson and Marcus, his partner, had large diamond interests, they were not at the moment realisable.

At about that time Alfred Beit, having foreseen the prospects of the gold discoveries on the Witwatersrand, was anxious to secure the services of a good man who would be capable of representing his firm there.

His choice fell on a German of the name of Hermann Eckstein, the manager of a Kimberley diamond mine, whom he had known intimately for some time. They had both belonged to what was then known in Kimberley as the Old German Mess, among whose members, beside Eckstein and Beit, were Henrichson, Martin Van Beek, and Julius Wernher.

Beit therefore proposed to Hermann Eckstein that he should found a branch of his firm in Johannesburg in order to handle all their Transvaal interests. Eckstein, however, had a good job at the time in Kimberley, and was not willing to give it up unless he could improve his position. Accordingly, he made the stipulation that he would like to visit the Transvaal with Beit before making up his mind.

* * *

It will be remembered that it was on my advice that Beit had sold out all his holdings in the Barberton district, and both he and Porges were not only grateful, but also realised that my years of experience in gold mining and my experience as a mine sampler would be of value to them.

They asked me what my plans were for the future, and I told them that I intended going to the Rand to establish myself there, as the prospects of a boom seemed rosy. They thereupon made me a counter-proposal, inviting me to join Hermann Eckstein in founding a branch of their firm on the Witwatersrand. The proposal was that we should come in on the ground floor and take over at cost for account of the firm, in which Eckstein and I were to have a participation, its one-third share in the Robinson Syndicate. Alfred Beit and Jules Porges undertook to provide all the funds required for this syndicate and also for any new business.

It was a very fine offer, and I knew it, but I was averse to having a partner, because I wanted to be free to do as I pleased, and I knew that I could do well on the Rand by myself. However, Beit, for whom I always had the deepest affection, impressed upon me that it was in my own interest that he was urging me to agree to his proposal. Eventually I gave

HERMANN ECKSTEIN

way, and we all travelled together to Pretoria and thence to the Witwatersrand.

Thus it came about that Hermann Eckstein and I founded the firm of 'Hermann Eckstein.' Our first building consisted of a wood and iron erection at the corner of Commissioner Street, now one of the busiest streets of Johannesburg. Then we substituted a brick building for the old rough and ready structure, and finally we built a two-storey building, which became known as 'The Corner House.'

When we became established we took over the management of the Robinson Syndicate and, subsequently, the flotation of the companies that had to be established in order to develop its various properties, such as the Langlaagte, the Langlaagte Block B, Randfontein, Bantjes, and Robinson mines.

It did not take me long to realise that my partner was not only a very agreeable companion with a broad outlook on life, but also a man whose good sterling qualities commanded universal respect. He was an able financier and a sound man of business; moreover, he very soon became the leading man on the Rand, whose interest and patronage were sought by all classes of the community. As a sportsman he did not shine, although he became the first President of the Wanderers Club, and of many other sporting societies in Johannesburg. Other branches of sport were left to me.

From the day we opened our doors to do business, Eckstein strove to maintain that high standard of honesty and business integrity which characterised the firm we were representing, and—I say it with pride—'The Corner House' has never departed from the standard we set up. It is a very fine record of which all those associated with the old firm may well be proud, for the temptations to get rich quick by crooked means were great.

* * *

In order to finance our various mining ventures it would have been quite impossible to rely entirely on support from London, because there the market for mining shares was too narrow. Very few of the big houses such as Rothschilds, Barings, or Schroeders took more than a passing interest in gold mining. They might have a flutter, but that was as far as it went. There was not enough speculative capital available in London for anything big. Alfred Beit saw from the start the magnitude of the financial support required by the Rand, and provided for it by obtaining Continental support.

As a result of the popularity that the De Beers shares had enjoyed in Paris, Berlin, and Vienna, the same groups which had introduced these shares on their respective exchanges fathered the gold shares offered to them by Wernher, Beit & Company, and in this way it became possible to sell in Paris as many as 100 000 shares in one deal. Thus Wernher, Beit & Company raised working capital for their mines, and did not have to resort to issuing prospectuses and soliciting public subscriptions. The shares placed on the Continent were well held, so that in any setback Wernher, Beit & Company had no moral obligation to repurchase shares that they had issued. Many of the failures of subsequent ventures floated in Johannesburg have been due to the fact that subscriptions were obtained in a narrow market.

Thus when Beit realised that it would be necessary to obtain the support of international financiers and bankers in order to raise all the capital required for the gold mining industry, he decided to broaden the market by giving participations to the Rothschilds of Germany, Austria, and France. Through Rudolph Kahn of Paris, he secured the support of many banking houses; in fact, all those houses which had made money out of diamond shares became eager to participate in gold shares. In reviewing the great mining industry of the Witwatersrand today, one should realise that it was through those channels that it originally received its chief support.

Our first flotation was called the Robinson Gold Mining Company. It had a capital of £50 000, of which £5 000 only was working capital. Japie De Villiers had 10 000 vendors' shares of £1 each, which he had received for his interest. We bought these shares from him at £8 per share, and they eventually went up to £100.

We then completed the flotation of the two Langlaagte properties, and also of the Randfontein and Bantjes mines.

We subsequently acquired interests belonging to Robinson and Marcus, including their interests in the Robinson Mine. For these assets we paid them £250 000.

When Robinson and Marcus received our cheque for £250 000, they declared that they had never seen a cheque for such a large amount in their lives. Robinson at once invited Eckstein and me to have a glass of champagne to celebrate the occasion. So we all adjourned to the Exchange bar, where Robinson ordered the wine.

Four glasses were poured out, and Robinson was just about to give the toast, while we were raising our glasses to our lips, when Abe Bailey strolled in. Robinson paused and shouted to Bailey, 'Come along, Abe, we are celebrating a big share transaction that I have just put through with Eckstein and Taylor. Come and join us.'

Taking Marcus's glass of champagne, he handed it to Bailey, saying, 'Marcus, you don't want any.'

As time passed, we decided, on the advice of our firm's technical advisers, to sell our interests in the mines situated west of Johannesburg, that is to say, in the Langlaagte, Langlaagte Block B, Bantjes, and the Randfontein mines, leaving J B Robinson in control. We had decided to stick to the Central and East Rand. In 1892 I bought the reversion of the Crown Mines *mynpacht* from J B Robinson, and it came about in the following way.

The Chairman of the Company, W H Rogers, asked me whether I would approach Robinson and try and bring about a deal. The directors of the Company had failed in their attempts. Rogers told me that the Crown Mines Company had to decide to buy the reversion or increase their plant, so as to work out the mine before the expiry of the lease, which had about ten years to run. The Company was prepared to pay £25 000 for this reversion. The next morning I saw Robinson standing talking to a man in the street, so I went over to him and asked him to spare me a few minutes on special business. I told him that the Crown Mines were on the point of deciding not to increase their milling capacity unless they could purchase the reversion of the lease, and I asked him whether he would take £25 000 for it. He asked me if I was empowered to deal on behalf of the Company and, on learning that I was, he replied, 'Are you sure they won't give more?'

I replied that it was the best price that he would get from me.

'Well,' he said, 'come over to Charlie Leonard's office and we will fix the matter up.'

Bailey Robinson Eckstein Taylor Marcus

When we arrived, he said to Leonard, 'Please drawn up a deed of sale. I have sold Taylor, on behalf of Crown Mines, the reversion rights of the *mynpacht* for £25 000.'

The present value is about as many millions.

About that time Rhodes and Beit obtained an option from Colonel Ferreira, Carl Hanau, and the Barbers to buy a block of claims, which subsequently became the Ferreira Mine, for £30 000. Before they could make up their minds to exercise the option, Beit asked me to sample the reef, so far as it was exposed. The deepest hole was not more than ten feet in depth. I was confident that I could form a very good estimate of the value of the reef, as I had not forgotten the experience I had gained at Lydenburg with the kind assistance of Gardner Williams.

We all happened to be staying in Pretoria: Rhodes, Beit, Porges, Gardner Williams, and I. After dinner, Gardner Williams asked me to go for a walk with him. It was a lovely moonlit night, and we sauntered up towards the open space on which the Pretoria railway station is now built. Williams said that he had asked me to come because he wanted my advice, since I knew all about the Kimberley Diamond Mines.

It appeared that Rhodes had offered him the General Managership of the De Beers Company, and he hesitated to accept it because it was such a big job, and he was uncertain whether he could give Rhodes satisfaction.

I pointed out to him that his qualifications were better than those of any mining engineer in the country, that the retiring general manager, Edward Jones, had not had anything like as much experience, and that he certainly ought to accept. We then walked back to the house, and as we came near he turned to me and said, 'Well, I suppose I'd better accept, but if I do I'll never look at a gold mine again.'

Early the next morning I went off to the Rand to the Ferreira Mine, took samples, and spent the evening assaying them. The next day, Rhodes, Beit, Porges, and Williams turned up at the mine to see the result of my sampling and decide whether they would exercise the option to buy or not.

Rhodes said, 'Well, Taylor, what do you make of it?'

I told him I had sampled the smaller of the two reefs, and that the average pannings checked by assay gave a return of from one to one-and-a-half ounces per ton of free milling gold. I showed him a lot of specimens with visible gold, and told him it was the most consistently rich lode I had yet sampled, but that I could not find payable values in the big main reef.

Rhodes then turned to Williams and said, 'Well, Williams, do you think this estimate is correct?'

Williams replied that he had taught me mine-sampling, and was confident that my report could be relied on. Rhodes admitted that the results were rich and, turning to Beit, asked him what he thought about exercising the option. Beit in turn asked Williams what he thought.

Here I saw my opportunity to pull Williams's leg, 'What's the good of asking Williams?' I said. 'He assured me two nights ago that he was never going to look at a gold mine again.' That raised a laugh all round.

Williams then went on to explain that he was quite satisfied that the lode I had sampled was rich enough to yield free milling gold for a depth of about one hundred to two hundred feet, but that then the nature of the ore would change and the gold would be found in sulphides. The free milling ore would then come to an end, and the treatment of the ore would have to be carried out by the only known method at that time, namely concentration of the sulphides by the frue-vanner process, and then by chlorination.

'This process is expensive,' Williams went on to say, 'and may possibly run into a cost of four pounds per ton. The cost of such a plant would also be heavy, and there does not appear to be any water available.'

Williams then assured us that he had no doubt that if a small mill were erected the mine would fully justify the purchase at the option price, because probably sufficient free gold would be recovered down to the sulphide level to give us our money back. But he gave it as his opinion that the proposition would not pay unless some cheaper method of working the sulphide ore could be devised. This threw a damper on the spirits of the party, as they had acquired many properties along the reef. They therefore decided not to exercise the Ferreira option.

* * *

After Eckstein and I had thoroughly established our business, and the shares of all the companies on the Rand began to soar, our firm started looking round for some more good mines, and I mentioned to Beit that I still held the opinion that the Ferreira Mine would turn out to be one of the Rand's richest mines. After we had allowed our option to lapse the owners had formed a company with a capital of £33 000; the vendors had taken £30 000 in shares, which left £3 000 for proving the mine.

The shares were then standing at 30s to 35s in the market, and we agreed that we should endeavour to obtain control. I therefore went into the market and bought out all the big holders. By the time I had completed the purchase of about 25 000 shares, the price had risen to 50s.

The Company's battery was erected near Auckland Park because there was water there. The ore was carted three miles from the mine to the battery in an ox wagon.

I joined the Board of the Company and attended the meetings, which were held in a small tent on the mine. The directors sat on gin-cases; and the general manager, Mr Grootgut Gutmann, sat on an upturned bucket. Mr Gutmann was a German miner, and spoke deep, gutteral English, prefacing all his remarks thus, 'Arrah gut, Mr Scharman and shentelmans.'

Needless to say, we soon dispensed with Mr Gutmann's services and, in fact, reconstructed the Board.

We then appointed Mr Harry Johns as general manager, and he drew up a complete plan for developing the mine and for a crushing plant of forty stamps. Our firm advanced the necessary capital to the extent of £90 000, and when the mine had been proved, the Company was reconstructed and the loan repaid. The profit of the Ferreira Mine, which had an issued capital of £95 000, was for many years £300 000 per annum.

* * *

In the good old 'boom' days of Johannesburg, companies, good and bad, were floated daily.

One day news came into the camp that rich ore had been found near the Rand to the south of the claim area, now belonging to the Crown Mines and that one of the big houses had bought the farm. Specimens of rich rock showing much visible gold were exhibited on the Stock

Exchange, and it was announced that the 'E' Company was in the course of formation to acquire the mine. There was great excitement over this new find because it was so far away to the south, off the strike of the outcrops of the conglomerate reefs running east and west.

The three partners in the concern met and decided that the capital of the company should be £100 000—half to the vendors and half working capital. The partners agreed that they would each sell 50 000 shares at a premium, and then meet at lunchtime to compare notes. When they met they found that they had sold shares in excess of the proposed capital. The senior partner of the group looked anxious for a moment, and then said, 'Did you tell them what the capital would be?'

'No, not a word about capital,' was the reply.

'Then go on selling,' said the senior partner, 'we will make the capital £200 000.'

The mine must have been salted, for no more gold-bearing rock ever came from that mine.

The senior partner was on his way to England, and voyaging in the same ship was a speculator, who had bought 4 000 of the shares at £2 premium. He tried hard every day to get in a word with the senior partner, but failed.

His chance came when going up the Channel. He cornered the senior partner, saying, 'Just a word. I want to ask you what you would do if you held 4 000 'E' shares costing you £3 a share?'

'Do,' came the reply, 'I would cut my bloody throat, so help me God!'

Chapter 10

The Mining Camp of Johannesburg

Before we built permanent residences in Johannesburg, Hermann Eckstein and I, together with several of our intimate friends, lived in rooms in a tin shanty. Next to us was a more imposing building, where we established what we called *The Decemveri Mess*.

Among the members I can remember the names of Harry Currey, manager of Rhodes's mining interests, Henri Bettleheim, whose nickname was 'Beetles,' a name known to every Johannesburger, Dr Hans Sauer, of whom the reader has already heard, John Scott, afterwards a judge in Rhodesia, and, of course, Hermann and Freddie Eckstein and myself. Alfred Beit and Cecil Rhodes were made honorary members, and always messed with us whenever they came to the Rand.

Frequently members of the mess who had been away for a few days would return with some game that they had shot on the veld. If anyone came home after a day on the veld without having remembered to replenish our larder, he was greeted with shouts of 'Didn't you shoot anything?' until he felt quite guilty if he came back with nothing.

Johnny Scott was one of those men who have a conscience. I knew that he was no sportsman and had had little to do with guns. I was therefore rather surprised when Johnny asked me to lend him some cartridges. I

CARTOONS BY WH SCHROEDER, 1891:
HERMANN ECKSTEIN (LEFT), JB TAYLOR (RIGHT)

asked him where his gun was, and he told me that he had borrowed one and was going out for a few days' shooting.

I must confess that I was rather nervous about his going out shooting alone, and as I handed him the cartridges I gave him a little advice. He took the former but scorned the latter.

About five o'clock, to my astonishment, Johnny rolled up with a broad grin on his face and a fine Egyptian goose fastened to his saddle. I did not show my surprise, but just told our cook to prepare the bird and roast it for dinner.

Just before it was served up, Johnny had begun a long story of how he had slain the bird. 'As soon as I spotted him,' he said, 'I crept as near as I could to him, and then as I got quite close I crawled nearer on my stomach. Suddenly I got up, because I wanted to give the bird a chance. At about twenty yards I brought him down the first shot.'

Here someone asked Johnny what size shot he had used. Johnny got very red and said, 'Number 4 shot.' As a matter of fact, when I had given him the cartridges I had told him they contained Number 4 shot.

Just at that moment someone held up a mushroomed bullet that he had found in a piece of goose on his plate.

'What on earth is this bullet doing in the bird, then?' he cried.

Poor Johnny had nothing to say. Then, at last, he confessed that he had bought the goose from a one-legged man called White who was in charge of a mine that he had been visiting.

We teased Johnny unmercifully after that, and he never really forgave us for finding him out.

* * *

At the same mess we had a German butler named Carl. Carl was a first-rate caterer, and never missed anything good on the morning market. Vegetables were a luxury in those days. I remember at a dinner party, when some of the *belles* of the town were gracing our board, Carl offered a dish of cauliflower to one of them. She declined, and Carl was struck with amazement. Surely she could not have understood him; there must be something wrong. He had been to the early morning market and had outbid all other buyers for this fine cauliflower; so he presented the dish again.

'No thanks,' said the lady once more.

'But,' said Carl, in a loud voice, 'it's cauliflower; it cost five shillings on the morning market.'

On another occasion Carl had made some caviar on toast, and had put a plate of it before me. As I did not eat caviar, I went on talking to Eckstein, who was sitting next to me. All the time I was talking, I was toying with my knife. Carl apparently thought that I was hesitating because I did not know what knife to use, and there was a roar of laughter when he lent over my shoulder and said, 'That's fish; use your fish-knife and fork.'

* * *

Once, when Rhodes visited the Rand he came to our mess-room as we were breakfasting, and when the meal was over he asked me to go for a walk with him. After a little while, to my surprise, he proposed that I should join him in purchasing from a Boer of the name of Bezuidenhout a farmhouse which lay in a pretty valley under the *kopje* to the east of Johannesburg, now known as Bezuidenhout Valley.

Rhodes suggested that we should buy this property on joint account, that we should pull down the old homestead, and build a nice house on the site for ourselves.

As I had seen booms and slumps in Kimberley, at Pilgrim's Rest, and at Barberton, Rhodes's proposal did not appeal to me. Moreover, I had no magnificent ideas about sharing a residence with him. Bezuidenhout would not sell, so nothing came of it.

* * *

At the time when Rhodes and Beit decided against exercising the option to buy the Ferreira Mine, I had not realised how deeply Rhodes had been impressed by the remarks made by Gardner Williams about the probable high cost of extracting gold from pyritic rock when, as prophesied by him, it would be encountered at a depth of about two hundred feet.

The lack of confidence shown by Rhodes in the future of the Rand continued to manifest itself for a long time. It is true that this may have arisen unconsciously in earlier days when he had not been invited by Robinson to participate in the original syndicate that had taken up so much of those portions of the Witwatersrand outcrops which were anticipated to yield the richest returns. All this may be accounted for by the fact that Rhodes and Robinson had never been very friendly to each other.

Therefore, when Rhodes arrived on the Rand he found that the Robinson Syndicate had already secured the pick of the properties that were for sale, and as he was not prepared to buy at high prices he cast around for interests in properties lying east and west of the Central Rand. At the time of which I write he was developing the Du Preez Reef, which afterwards became the Rietfontein Mine.

Although Rhodes had no enthusiasm for gold mining, and looked upon it entirely as a sideline compared with diamond mining, he disliked the feeling of not having a finger in every pie. Besides, he was never averse from making money whenever there was a chance.

In addition to the many difficulties of gold extraction, which presented themselves to his mind, Rhodes's Kimberley experience told him that mining required much water, and he could not see where the water was going to come from.

He was confident that he had in the De Beers Company one of the biggest mining undertakings in the world, and at the same time he had at the back of his mind the conviction that his next great work was to be the development of the unknown riches of the country north of the Transvaal.

Nevertheless, he did acquire some interests on the Rand and laid the foundations for the mining operations subsequently undertaken by a company which he named 'The Consolidated Goldfields of South Africa.'

Rhodes never ceased trying to wean Alfred Beit away from the lure of the Rand.

'It will never do,' he thought, 'to let Beit forget that his diamond interests are calling him. If Beit becomes too deeply involved in this gold business I may risk losing his support, which I absolutely need for the fulfilment of my dreams in the north and the acquisition of the political power that I must have behind me when the moment arrives.'

MR AND MRS HERMANN ECKSTEIN

Rhodes used to try to persuade even me to influence Beit to curtail his financial obligations on the Rand. He left Hermann Eckstein alone. They never liked one another.

It was never out of Rhodes's mind that it was Beit's money, and the money interests that Beit could 'influence,' that were the chief props of the diamond industry. He realised that Beit's following among the German, Austrian, and French bankers was very strong, and that through these sources almost unlimited capital was at Beit's command.

'Would not the capital required for the mines which were to be floated by the Robinson Syndicate have to come from these sources? No prospectuses would be necessary, and the money required would be found among Beit's friends.' These were the lines along which Rhodes's thoughts ran.

One day I received an invitation from Rhodes to spend the day with him on the Du Preez Mine, where at that time he was living. He had a small house there with an annexe. His other guests were C D Rudd, his partner, and his brother Frank, who was then a captain in a cavalry regiment, and best remembered as Colonel Rhodes.

The Du Preez Mine was doing badly, and Rhodes was beginning to think that it was a sample of what all Rand gold mines would turn out to be.

After dinner we sat talking till about eleven o'clock, when we had a final drink before turning in. Rhodes brought a candle and showed me to my room in the annexe, and after saying, 'Good night,' went off to his own room. I was very tired, and no sooner had I got into bed than I fell asleep.

About 2 am I heard my door open, and who should come into my room but Rhodes in his dressing gown, with a candle in his hand. For two solid hours he sat on my bed declaiming against Rand gold mines, and declaring that the only mining worth undertaking was diamond-mining on the property owned by the De Beers Company. He kept on repeating, in his high-pitched voice, that we ought to seize the opportunity to sell all our gold-mining interests and return to Kimberley, because the amalgamation of the mines which had recently taken place assured greater security for capital, and much larger fortunes could be made there.

It began to dawn on my sleepy brain that Rhodes was visualising that 'The Corner House' would grow into something very big and devote all its resources to the development of its Transvaal interests. He must do everything in his power to prevent his able lieutenant, Alfred Beit, from wandering away from his control and devoting his firm's capital to furthering interests in which he, Rhodes, had no share.

While he was in my room he talked on, but I cannot recall all that he said because, as I say, I was half asleep most of the time. All I know is that he kept trying to hammer into my head what a much bigger thing the De Beers Mine was than anything on the Rand was ever likely to be. I, for my part, was convinced that he was wrong and I tried to tell him so, but he would have none of it. I felt strongly that while his one idea seemed to be to induce me to advise Alfred Beit not to go too deeply into gold mining, he did not care what happened to Eckstein and me and the firm we represented.

Chapter 11

Johannesburg Grows

When the township of Johannesburg was being surveyed, Hermann Eckstein and I decided to build brick houses for ourselves, and we commenced looking about for sites. The town had been laid out as far as the present road facing what is now Park Station. This was the northern boundary of the town, and we felt pretty certain that no one would build in front of us. We had a clear view of the *kopje* to the north where the *Fort* now stands, and in the summer the green grass and bushes grew between the rocks.

People seemed to think that we were very optimistic about the future of the goldfields because we were putting up such permanent buildings. Their curiosity was aroused to such a pitch that they used to take Sunday walks to see what progress our buildings were making.

Our houses were not completed when the first pyritic rock was struck at 180 feet in depth in the City and Suburban Mine. I then remembered what Gardner Williams had prophesied.

Eckstein and I consulted our experts, and as they agreed that the expense of treating the pyritic ore on the Rand would be about double the cost of treating the oxidised or free milling ore, we began to think that perhaps the outlook was not so rosy after all.

PARK HALT, LATER JOHANNESBURG STATION, 1892, WITH ECKSTEIN AND TAYLOR'S HOUSES IN THE BACKGROUND

We therefore cabled to our head office in London, asking if we should continue our building operations. The reply was not long delayed.

Beit, whose confidence in the Rand could never be shaken, replied, 'Yes, by all means.' So these bungalows of ours, with their corrugated-iron roofs, were completed, and when I was last on the Rand they still stood facing Park Railway Station, looking like pioneers by the side of the present-day skyscrapers.

When we had settled in we had the usual housewarming and made ourselves thoroughly comfortable. In my house I had a billiard table and a nice bathroom with hot and cold water.

I have mentioned my 'boy' Shilling, the Shangaan, who had been with me all the time that I lived in the Barberton and Lydenburg districts. He was still my faithful servant when I settled down in Johannesburg, and as a reward I dressed him up in white clothes and made him my butler.

I had an old Scotch cook, a very good woman, except that she could not stand Shilling, whom she always called 'that grinning black baboon.' She was continually complaining to me about Shilling's evil doings, and said she was sure that he was in the habit of using my bath.

One day a friend of mine came to my house and asked me if he might have a bath, as baths were rather scarce in the early days of Johannesburg. I showed him where the bathroom was, but I made the fatal mistake of not telling the cook, who heard my friend splashing away in the water, and immediately jumped to the conclusion that it must be my 'boy' Shilling.

Here was the opportunity she had been waiting for. Stamping down the passage, she was heard to say, 'You grinning black baboon, I've caught yer, have I, and the master said you didn't do it.' Whereupon she flung the bathroom door open, and there she found my poor friend cowering in the bath.

As we wanted to make doubly sure that there would never be any buildings in front of us to spoil our view, although at the time we had not the faintest idea that eventually the railway station would be planked down a few yards from our fence, we conceived the idea of working up a demand for a large playground for the town, which would be in front of our houses.

FIRST COMMITTEE OF WANDERERS CLUB, 1889
HERMANN ECKSTEIN AND JB TAYLOR ARE SEATED IN THE CENTRE

It was suggested that we should get up a deputation to go over to Pretoria to interview President Kruger and formally lay our request before him. The idea was to secure fifty or sixty acres of ground in front of our houses and convert it into a sports club.

The deputation consisted of many of those who were interested in obtaining the concession over the ground for this club, and included Llewellyn Andersson, Jacob Swart, Eckstein, and myself.

It was quite a journey to Pretoria in those days of horses and carts, but eventually we arrived at Paul Kruger's house. After the deputation had been introduced, the object of our mission was explained to the President, and much stress was laid on the need of the Johannesburg public for a playing-ground in order to divert their mind from politics.

A sketch of the size was produced, but when the President saw the size of the ground required, he demurred, saying that the loss of revenue to the State if such a large area were devoted to a playground instead of being sold as town plots would be considerable. Finally, however, the President said, 'This is a matter for the Minister of Mines and the Mining Commissioners to decide. You had better go and see them.'

We then got up and thanked the President, shook hands all round, and set off to find Joubert.

Christiaan Joubert, Kruger's Minister of Mines, was a grey-bearded old *takhaar* Boer; he was a cousin of Frans Joubert, who had forced the surrender of Colonel Anstruther's column at Bronkhorstspruit in 1880.

After we had discussed the whole matter with the Minister, and thought we had convinced him, he raised a lot of difficulties.

'I shall have to go to the Rand,' he said, 'to see what you want, and how do you expect me to get there? I have no cart and horses, and unless I can inspect the ground and satisfy myself that your demands are reasonable, I cannot give my consent.'

Obviously it was a question of cart and horses. I therefore said, 'Would it help you, General, if we provided the cart and horses? We in Johannesburg feel strongly the need of seeing more of our Minister of Mines, because there are so many important problems to be solved on the spot in a new township like Johannesburg, where there is always the possibility of the interests of the town and the mines clashing.'

After some moments of deep thought, old Joubert looked up.

'Yes,' he said, 'that would probably be a solution.'

JB TAYLOR

I immediately seized the opportunity and replied, 'Would it suit the Minister to receive the cart and horses on Thursday next, and would the Minister drive over to Johannesburg on Friday?'

'*Ja, ja*,' said the old man, and after much handshaking we parted, feeling pretty certain that our request would be granted.

On the appointed Thursday a beautiful new Cape cart with glittering harness and a pair of milk-white horses appeared before the Minister's front door in Pretoria, and on the next day he drove over to Johannesburg.

We were on the lookout for him, and received him with grateful thanks. We took him at once to the site that we required, and he made the necessary inspection, asking many questions.

When he had looked at the plan and satisfied himself that it corresponded with the land that we wanted, he seemed to think that it was incumbent upon him to say a few words. He therefore addressed the members of the deputation and, much to our amusement and satisfaction, he told us how necessary it was for the health of the youth of the town that there should be a recreation ground. He concluded by telling us that the piece of land for which we had asked would be reserved for that purpose, and that the grant would be made to a properly constituted body at a 'peppercorn rent.'

That was how the Wanderers Club was formed, with Hermann Eckstein as its first Chairman and myself as Vice-chairman. I have a photograph of the members of the first Committee.

Although we had secured an open space in front of our houses, we did not enjoy this for very long, for the building of the railway from Johannesburg to Delagoa Bay was even then being contemplated, and the surveyors were proposing to bring the line right in front of our doors, between us and the Wanderers Club ground. We did our best to get the route altered, but failed.

At the time our technical advisers were strongly of the opinion that the railway line should have been taken along the line of reef with sidings to the mines.

Chapter 12

Our Technical Staff

It will be remembered that when the Rand goldfields were discovered in 1886-7, little was known about gold mining in South Africa. Gold was being recovered from alluvial deposits in the Lydenburg and Pilgrim's Rest districts, and in a small way from reefs in Barberton, but the results did not justify the employment of highly paid engineers.

By far the most experienced gold-mining engineer in South Africa at that time was Gardner Williams, who, as the reader will remember, was employed by the Transvaal Gold Mining and Estates Company at Pilgrim's Rest when I was working there. He was an efficient gold miner, but, as I have recorded, from the day that Rhodes made him general manager of the De Beers Diamond Mine he steadfastly refused to have anything more to do with gold mining.

When our firm had established 'The Corner House' in Johannesburg, we were faced with the problem of obtaining the best possible men for the development of our mines.

After talking the matter over with Beit, Eckstein and I decided that the first thing we had to do was to engage a consulting engineer of the highest qualifications in order to bring the gold mines under our control to the producing stage as efficiently as possible.

We at once sought the advice of Gardner Williams, who assured us that the ablest men for our purpose were to be found in America, where gold mining had been carried on for years on a large scale and where the best machinery, such as that manufactured by Messrs Fraser and Chalmers, could be obtained.

After thinking the matter over, Gardner Williams recommended us to get in touch with two well-known mining engineers named respectively Hamilton Smith and De Crano, who were frequently consulted by the Rothschilds and enjoyed the entire confidence of the partners of that firm. We followed Williams's advice, with the result that we were strongly recommended, if possible, to get hold of the manager of the El Calao Mine in Venezuela, a man of the name of Hennen Jennings, who had a great reputation as a mining engineer. Under him, working on the same mine, was Colonel Cresswell, who later on came to the Rand and became a mine manager.

After an exchange of letters, Hennen Jennings agreed to enter our employ, and no one can deny that his arrival in South Africa was one of the lucky events that blessed the fortunes of 'The Corner House.'

When the time came to erect our first milling plant we wrote, on Jennings's advice, to Messrs Fraser and Chalmers in America, with whom our orders were placed, asking them if they would send us a first-class mechanical engineer.

The reply came back to the effect that we could not do better than employ Judd Coppach, whom they had originally sent out to erect the plant at the Lisbon-Berlin Mine at Lydenburg.

I had acquired a great liking for Judd, especially since he had bearded Baron Grant in the Baron's office in London, and demanded his pay. We therefore wrote to Judd asking him to join us. We never regretted the step.

Judd was a great character, popular with everyone. He was an ardent poker player, and one of his cronies who used to play with him was Dr Matthews, formerly a well-known Kimberley doctor. Matthews had married the sister of J Bryant Lindley, who represented in South Africa the Equitable Insurance Company of America. As a sideline, the doctor acted as agent for his brother-in-law, and tried to persuade Judd to take out a tontine life policy.

HENNEN JENNINGS

After Matthews had explained this system of life insurance at great length, Judd suddenly looked up and said, 'Cut it short, Doctor. I want to know where I come in.'

'Listen, Judd,' said Matthews, 'when you die the Company has to pay——'

'Hold hard,' said Judd, 'what do you mean when you say that if I die the Company has to pay? No, thank you, I'll never play a game at which I have to die to win.'

* * *

Just as Judd Coppach proved to be exactly the right mechanical engineer for us, so did Hennen Jennings show himself to be a man of outstanding ability as a mining engineer, for everyone liked him and his men liked working under him. We soon found that he was the best man we could have engaged for the great task that we set before him. From the beginning he realised the magnitude of the discoveries that had been made on the Rand, and the possibility of laying the foundation for their development on a bigger scale and under more efficient methods than had ever been attempted by any other mining enterprise.

After thoroughly surveying and sampling the properties under our control, he gave us plans and specifications for the work to be done, the right kind of machinery to be ordered, and he secured for us the best men to carry out the work. In fact, we gave him a free hand and footed the bill.

Jennings imported the best mine captain he had known in America in the person of Captain Mein, who agreed to come to South Africa to take over the management of the Robinson Mine from Frank Spencer, who subsequently discovered and managed the Bonanza Mine. Mein arrived with his wife and family, and we built them a comfortable house on the mine.

Jennings also engaged an American metallurgist called Charles Butters of California, whose name afterwards became known all over the world in mining circles. Butters erected a chlorination plant for us on the Robinson Mine, and was able by this means to extract the gold from the frue-vanner concentrates economically until the cyanide process became universal.

Men such as J R Williams, George Webber, H C Perkins, and Louis Irving Seymour became famous on the Rand, and the good work they did set an example that was followed by others. They were all employees of 'The Corner House,' I am proud to say, and contributed to the establishment of the reputation that the Rand possessed the most efficiently run gold-mining industry in the world.

It is entirely due to Hennen Jennings that no mistakes were made either in the layout of our mines or the method employed for the extraction of gold. Having a grasp of the magnitude of the undertaking, he introduced the most modern methods of working the mines economically. He kept himself *au fait* with what was being done in other mining centres, continually making improvements until, for efficiency, the mines under his control had no rivals in any other mining centre.

And yet, Jennings's work has never been sufficiently appreciated in South Africa. Never was there a man who more surely deserved a tribute to his memory in grateful appreciation of what he did for the country.

Many good mining engineers followed Hennen Jennings on the Rand, men whose names will always be remembered in the annals of the Rand mining industry, but it was Jennings and the men he employed who blazed the trail. They set an example to the world of how good, honest mining should be carried on, and they did it at a time when gold mining was rightly looked upon with distrust by most investors.

From the start Alfred Beit laid down a stern command to our firm that the shareholders were to receive a monthly report of the progress made on all the mines we controlled, good, bad, or indifferent. Nothing was withheld. This practice was also followed by other groups, and has continued ever since, with the result that in no other country in the world are shareholders so fully informed and supplied with such regular and accurate information.

This has always been appreciated on the stock exchanges of the world, where Rand shares have had a free market and have been popular counters ever since the mines were placed on a permanent footing.

* * *

One of the properties that Hennen Jennings advised us to acquire was the Modderfontein Farm. He began the exploratory work by putting in long cross-cuts in order to ascertain the lie of the reef until the site of the first shaft could be located.

As we were spending money on a part of the Rand so far away to the east, on a part of the outcrop more or less unexplored, we had to give the work our close attention. Hermann Eckstein and I used to visit this property every Sunday to inspect the work done during the week.

On the occasion of one of our visits to Modderfontein, Sigismund Newmann said that he would like to come with us. It was wintertime and the weather was very cold. Our vehicle was an American spider with the hood let down. Neumann and Eckstein sat behind and I sat next to the driver with a rifle between my knees, for in those days *pauw* and other game were often found near the road that ran parallel with the reef, and I never gave up hope of bringing home some game for our mess.

All went well till we reached a marshy bit of ground ten or twelve miles from Johannesburg. As soon as I saw what we were in for I told the driver to whip up his horses and take it at a gallop. He did what he was told, and as the horses leapt forward Neumann leaned over and clutched at the reins, imploring the driver not to go so fast. The two leading horses had just reached the soft ground and I could tell that it was swampy. It needed only that momentary indecision on the part of the man who held the reins to put the fear into them that the ground was not safe. So round they came in a flash. I saw at once what was going to happen, and jumped out with the intention of seizing the horses' bridles, but I got mixed up in my long overcoat and took a toss. Before I could recover myself all four horses had turned right round and bolted.

I shall never forget what followed. At full gallop the horses careered over the veld. As the spider threaded the scattered ant-heaps, it struck first one and then another, so that there were never more than two wheels on the ground at a time. The hood, too, was flapping up and down.

As I was getting up from the ground I saw one fat leg appearing over the back of the hood, then another, then a big fat back, then spasmodic grabs to get a holding, and down flopped Eckstein on to the ground.

By this time I had discarded my overcoat and was racing hard after the spider. I found Eckstein unhurt, but was horrified to see Neumann trying to get out. First I saw a leg put out and then withdrawn; then a big ant-heap caught the two near wheels and turned the spider upside down, the horses bolting off with pole and traces.

The driver was thrown clear and was unhurt, but we could see that Neumann must be underneath the cart, and we thought he must be killed, for he made no sound.

We quickly turned the cart over and, pulling Neumann out, we propped him up against some cushions. Luckily, we had some brandy with us, and we gave him a drink—till then he had only groaned, and could tell us nothing. We felt him all over and, finding no bones broken, we gave him time to recover.

All he could say was, 'I've had enough! I want to go home.'

I walked over to a farm nearby and found a Dutch boy with a cart already inspanned. After a little talk and the promise of a reward, I got him to agree to drive Neumann back to Johannesburg. We then went after our horses and, finding them unhurt, we hitched them onto the spider as well as we could and resumed our journey.

In the evening when we got home we went to see how Neumann was. We found him propped up in bed with the best black eye I have ever seen outside a prize ring. We asked him how he got this awful black eye, and he told us that he had been sitting dozing in the springless mule-cart behind the farm boy, when they went over a bad bump. Unfortunately, at that moment he was leaning forward on his gold-knobbed walking stick, which had hit him in the eye.

* * *

Besides my various duties in Johannesburg as Chairman of our gold-mining companies, to say nothing of having to direct the affairs of the Langlaagte and Randfontein companies to oblige J B Robinson during his absence in England, Eckstein and I took a responsible part in the development of the Wanderers Club. We also helped to form the Rand Club, in which we took up most of the debentures. It fell to my lot to found the Rand Rifle Association, and after getting together a few enthusiasts, we held our first meeting at Zoccola's Hotel in Johannesburg for the purpose of electing officers. They elected me President. I remember being much amused when Ewald Esselen turned up at this meeting with the only object of reporting to the Government whether or not this club was likely to be the forerunner of sinister designs.

It also fell to my lot to form one of the largest land companies in the Transvaal. The story of its origin is of historical interest.

In the Transvaal Republic military and other services rendered to the State were rewarded by grants of land known as 'Burgher Rights.' For instance, a man who went out 'on commando' was entitled to a farm. All he had to do was to go to his veld-cornet and ask where his farm was.

A tract of land was then selected by the veld-cornet, whose business it was to measure it roughly. His method was to ride for a certain distance in one direction, and then as nearly as possible at right angles in another direction. Beacons were not located, but a record was kept of the approximate positions in which such beacons would eventually have to be located.

Thus were these areas roughly defined and pieces of paper called 'inspection reports' signed by the veld-cornet were given to the grantees.

I remember how the boundaries of a farm called *Doornkloof* were described in a report:

> 'East of the spot where *Oom* Piet shot the springbok; one hour on horseback from there to the north beacon, which is on the hill where we made some coffee; one hour on horseback from there to the western boundary where we saw the meerkats.'

Other inspection reports described the corner of a farm as 'the place where we outspanned,' or 'the spot where the wagon wheel came off,' or 'the tree near which we shot a wildebeest and hung its horns up in the branches.'

George Pigot-Moodie, who, as I have already recorded, had been employed as surveyor by the Transvaal Government, had on one occasion given evidence in a case in Natal. It was about the beacon of a farm he had surveyed which had been fixed in the fork of a big tree amongst thick forest growth.

The Court appointed two men to visit the forest to see if the tree and the beacon could be located. After a long search Moodie eventually found the tree, but the growth of so many years had completely covered the stone, and it had to be cut away in order to reveal the beacon and prove the case to the satisfaction of the Court.

Sometimes, after receiving from the veld-cornet their titles in the form of slips of paper, grantees of farms took them to the nearest wayside store and sold them for a mere song. These chits changed hands by the dozen. The owner of the store, in his turn, having collected a certain number of such 'inspection reports,' would sell them to speculators and land companies.

I once saw a man in a bar in Pretoria pull out of his pocket sheaves of 'inspection reports,' and heard him offer to sell a parcel of ten farms of 6 000 acres each for £50 apiece. It can well be imagined, therefore, that land in the Transvaal at that time was very cheap.

My firm bought about three million acres in the Zoutspanberg, Waterberg and Lichtenberg districts, and formed a company which we called the 'Transvaal Consolidated Land Company,' of which I became Chairman and Managing Director.

The title deeds of this company's properties consisted of a lot of scraps of paper describing the farms as having been inspected by Veld-Cornet So-and-so. I therefore employed my cousin, Major Theodore Menne, as representative of the company and inspector of its properties, instructing him to go round with the veld-cornet of each district concerned and erect beacons as best he could. When the general survey of the country took place, he was able to point out our beacons to the surveyors.

Naturally there were many disputes and lawsuits, which led to the historic words spoken by Judge Kotze when he described farm boundaries as 'those roving beacons.'

My task was to see that all our farm titles were in order. This entailed many visits to the office of the Registrar of Deeds in Pretoria where Koos Meintjies and Hans Minnaar presided. Hans was a veritable encyclopaedia. He kept a complete record of every acre of land in the Transvaal. He could, without reference to his books, tell you who had sold or exchanged any farm you liked to name.

'*Ach, Mitalfallen,*' he would say, 'you mean the farm next to *Sterkspruit* that was last exchanged for a wagon and ten oxen by Piet van Tonder. Subsequently gold was found on that farm, and it was recently bought by the Hottentot Syndicate for £50 000.'

We settled natives as tenants and squatters on our company's farms. This helped to pay for the administration, and by this method caretakers were established on the land.

* * *

Our interests called for frequent visits to Pretoria, and on these occasions I generally called upon the President at his house. *Oom* Paul, as we used to call the President, liked me. He knew he could trust me.

At that period many adventurers were busy trying to persuade the Swazi king, M'bandini, to grant them concessions, or rather monopolies, to do, or make, or sell any conceivable thing.

Kruger was very anxious to annexe Swaziland for the Transvaal, and he was clever enough to see that if he could acquire the railway concession or the telegraph concession, it would help him to obtain a footing in that country.

He badly wanted £30 000 in order to buy some monopolies from one or two of the concessionaires. He therefore sent for me and asked if my firm would lend him the money at five per cent interest.

We decided that we would lend him the money, and agreed that the transaction be kept secret. However, we had to have some signed agreement, and I had one drawn up for the President's signature.

He was sitting at his table as I entered his sitting room with the document. I read the terms to him, and as I was handing him his pen he turned round and looked me in the face.

'This is a very secret agreement,' he said. 'Do you think that I can trust you?'

I frowned at him, and said, 'President, how can you say such a thing? Do you remember the boy sitting on the bed in Nicolaas Smit's room while you were discussing the terms of your petition which you wanted to put before Queen Victoria? Do you remember old Dr Jorrison asking you whether it was wise to discuss secret matters in front of me? Didn't you say then that you could trust me? Can't you trust me now?'

The President was overjoyed.

'Were you the boy?' he gasped.

'Yes, President, I was.'

With that he snatched the pen out of my hand and laboriously signed his name.

*　*　*

PRESIDENT PAUL KRUGER

At this stage in my story, I must record an event that made my life really worth living. I married 'the one woman in the world.'

This is how it came about. When I was twenty-two years of age, I happened to be visiting Natal. There I had the good fortune to meet Miss Mary (Mollie) Gordon, daughter of Dr Gordon, a well-known physician of Pietermaritzburg, Natal. I caught sight of her first in Greytown, just as she was taking her seat in the post-cart for Pietermaritzburg. My cousin, Doré Menne, and I were there to see the mail off, which was one of the principal events of the day.

Doré introduced me to Miss Gordon, who had been spending a holiday in Greytown. There was no opportunity for conversation with her because the post-cart was on the point of starting, and some of her friends had come to say goodbye to her; but it was a case of love at first sight with me, and I made up my mind that when I became well off enough to marry I would ask her to share my life with me.

In 1889 I resolved to visit England, and on the way to the coast I stopped at Pietermaritzburg for a few days, in the hope of renewing my acquaintance with Miss Gordon. She told me that she was leaving shortly to reside in Johannesburg, and I told her that I hoped to meet her again when I returned from Europe.

When I came back to Johannesburg the following year I asked her to marry me, and was accepted. We were married on 10 March 1891.

This was the beginning of a long and happy partnership such as few married couples have the luck to enjoy. Wherever we have made a home, Mollie has won the hearts of the people among whom we have lived. To this day, they have not forgotten her sympathy and acts of kindness whenever they were in trouble or in need.

Our four children adore their mother and look upon her as their dearest friend. There exists no better foundation for a happy family.

AGNES CUNNINGHAM, LEFT, AND MARY GORDON, RIGHT, IN PIETERMARIZBURG. AGNES CUNNINGHAM MARRIED SIR MICHAEL RIMINGTON OF THE 6TH INNISKILLING DRAGOONS, AND MARY GORDON MARRIED THE AUTHOR JB TAYLOR.

Chapter 13

Nellmapius, the President's Friend, Concessions and Monopolies

In the 'seventies a remarkable man arrived in the Transvaal from Austria. His name was Alois Hugo Nellmapius. He was a man of strong personality, and he had not been long in the country before President Kruger became attracted by him.

Personal bravery is a trait that always excites admiration in the eyes of people who lead adventurous lives, and Nellmapius was certainly a brave man. Especially had he earned Paul Kruger's respect during the fights that were in those days constantly taking place with native tribes in the Transvaal.

On one occasion, when Kruger, as Commandant of the burgher forces, led his men against the stronghold of the native chief, Mapoch, Nellmapius showed remarkable bravery, volunteering to lead when others were inclined to waver.

The stories of Nellmapius's bravery were well known to everybody. Colonel David Forbes, for instance, told me that he had served with 'Nelly,' as he called him, in the Sekukuni War, and a braver man he had never met. He told me that he once saw Nellmapius crawl up to the entrance of the caves in which the Kaffirs were located and throw dynamite charges with short fuses into the entrance. In these days we would call this bomb throwing.

It came about, therefore, that Kruger learnt to lean on this interesting man, and made him welcome at the Presidency whenever he chose to call, day or night.

Nellmapius had a good technical education, and his ambitions lay in industrial activity. He realised that in a young country industry could only be started if concessions could be obtained from the Government, granting the sole right to manufacture.

The first concession that Nellmapius managed to obtain from the President was granted to him in 1881, when he received the sole right to manufacture gunpowder. This monopoly he sold to a London-Amsterdam company called the Pioneer Factory, for which he received a block of shares. He also became Managing Director. One condition attached to the monopoly was that the Transvaal Government had the first call on all the gunpowder produced.

It is said that the European management frequently left Nellmapius without sufficient funds for improvements and the purchase of raw materials, and he claimed that he was often obliged to finance the company out of his own pocket.

Eventually the company's accounts became very involved, and some of the directors in Amsterdam protested that Nellmapius had robbed the company of £3 000.

In 1885 these directors decided to take criminal proceedings against poor Nellmapius, and finally persuaded their compatriot, Dr Leyds, the Transvaal State Attorney, to prosecute. Nellmapius's defence was that the Company owed him £8 500.

The trial dragged on for a year and was adversely criticised by the Press, which described it as 'persecution.' In spite of this Nellmapius was condemned to eighteen months' imprisonment.

This case is remarkable in that it demonstrates the autocratic powers assumed by President Kruger, who immediately granted a free pardon to Nellmapius and callously accepted the resignation of Judge Brand, who had pronounced the sentence. Subsequently Chief Justice Kotze reviewed the case and found that the President had acted strictly within his rights.

There was no doubt whatever in the minds of Eckstein and myself that Nellmapius was innocent of the charges that had been brought against him, for he was able to prove to our complete satisfaction that although he had been careless in keeping his accounts, mostly owing to the fact that the checking in the overseas office was very badly supervised, the company was indebted to him to the extent of much more than £3 000.

Our firm had very extensive dealings with Nellmapius after this unfortunate event, and his honesty and integrity were never once in doubt.

When I first met him I was at once impressed by his boundless energy, and no one could help being attracted by his implicit belief in the future of the country of his adoption. He could easily have amassed a fortune had he not been strictly honest in all his doings, and it is sad to have to relate that he died a poor man. He was a keen agriculturist, and his head was full of schemes for the furtherance of the industrial development of the country.

Money had only one use in Nellmapius's eyes. It was but a means by which he could develop his ideas. He secured, through his great influence over the President, the monopoly for the manufacture of spirit from maize and transferred the right to exploit this concession to Mr Sammy Marks, who was also one of Kruger's trusted friends.

Eckstein and I soon realised that Nellmapius was such a power in the land that we ought to make an effort to secure his co-operation on behalf of the mining industry of the Witwatersrand. He was, however, of a very retiring nature, and at first resisted all our advances, giving us the impression that he suspected that our activities were prompted solely by self-interest.

Gradually, however, when subsequently I had settled in Pretoria, he and I became great friends, and it was through his influence that I became the recognised intermediary in all negotiations between the mines and the Government, and was accepted by Kruger and his Executive Council as a friend upon whose services they could rely.

* * *

On one occasion I called upon the President and found him sitting as usual on his *stoep* drinking coffee, smoking and chatting with one or two members of the *Volksraad*.

After I had shaken hands all round, the President said to me, 'Come here, I want to speak to you. Why do you do so much for Johannesburg and so little for Pretoria? I think it is time that you did something for this place.'

'But, President,' I replied, 'you do not want my help. Look at all the concessions that you have given away to other people, such as the Pretoria waterworks, the Pretoria lighting, cement-making and banking concessions.'

'That is true,' replied the President, 'but your firm ought to take an interest in them and help the concessionaires to obtain the money they require.'

I listened to all he had to say, and then told him that I would discuss it with my firm. When next I saw Alfred Beit I mentioned the matter to him. He reminded me that our firm had always opposed concessions and monopolies. However, after further discussion, we came to the conclusion that as the concessions had already been granted we might well do something to start them going. He remarked that it would entail an obligation upon me to take up my residence in Pretoria and open an office there. To this I agreed.

In making this proposal to me, it was in Beit's mind that it would be a good plan to have a partner of the firm resident in Pretoria in order that he might act as the intermediary between the mines and the Government, and keep both parties informed of everything that was going on. I performed this function as well as I could until I left Pretoria. It was, in my opinion, a great misfortune for our firm, and indeed for the rest of the mining industry as a whole, that this practice was not continued.

It was partly owing to Paul Kruger's insistence and partly to show Nellmapius that we were in earnest in our desire to lend a hand in the development of the industrial enterprise of the country that my firm agreed to take over and help to finance the establishment of a National Bank and a State Mint, the manufacture of cement, and also the installation of electric light and the supply of water for the town of Pretoria.

I opened my office on behalf of the firm in a small cottage at the back of the present premises of Barclays Bank D, C & O (formerly the National Bank) in Pretoria, and became established as the Chairman of the various concerns which we had agreed to finance.

The fact that I can claim to be not only the founder of these various enterprises, but also to have brought them to a successful issue, is one of my most pleasant memories.

* * *

I would like here to record a certain episode that had in some degree influenced our firm in taking over the establishment of the then National Bank.

The concession for the formation of a National Bank and a State Mint had been granted to a group of financiers in Holland. They were Hope, Labouchere, Oyens & Company of Amsterdam, who had managed to obtain this monopoly through their fellow countryman, Dr Leyds, at that time Kruger's financial adviser.

Having failed to obtain the necessary capital after having hawked the concession about in Europe without success, the concessionaires deputed my old associate Edouard Lippert to try to float a company in the Transvaal.

One day Hermann Eckstein on returning from a board meeting of the Crown Reef Gold Mining Company entered my office in a furious temper, because the company had been refused an overdraft for £25 000 by its bankers.

Something had to be done, because, although our firm was always willing to lend money to any of our concerns, we did not see why we should furnish all the financial requirements of the mines under our control.

After talking the matter over we decided to lend the company the money it required. On the other hand, the action of the bank set us thinking. If the bankers of a producing gold-mining company could take up this attitude and refuse to grant temporary facilities, the gold-mining industry might be seriously embarrassed.

Thus it became evident that in order to obtain any sort of financial security in the future, a bank must be created for the purpose of supporting mining and industrial undertakings. The only question that exercised our minds was whether we should create a bank of our own or acquire Labouchere's concession for the establishment of a National Bank. I reminded Eckstein of the fact that Kruger was clamouring for a National Bank, and had already asked me to approach the concessionaires.

Eckstein agreed that this presented one way out of the predicament, but hated the idea of having anything to do with Lippert, because Lippert at that time was the head of a clique that was bleeding the gold-mining industry white through their dynamite monopoly.

I was therefore deputed to see what could be done. Eckstein stipulated that Lippert was to have nothing to do with the bank beyond the function of intermediary between the concessionaires and ourselves.

I found Lippert quite willing to come to terms and prepared to hand over the concession to us provided that we found all the capital required and that he and his friend received some founders' shares.

The capital of the National Bank was fixed at £1 000 000, the Government of the Transvaal Republic agreeing to take up £100 000. When it became known in Europe that our firm was connected with the flotation, the Deutsche Bank, the Dresdener Bank (through Messrs J H Schroeder of London), the Berliner Handel Gesellschaft, Messrs Labouchere Oyens and Messrs Hope offered to take participations.

As soon as the capital had been subscribed, my firm having taken up £100 000, Lippert, the Government's nominee, and I met in my office in Pretoria. We soon settled all the details. Like all our firm's undertakings, the issue was a private one, the public not being invited to participate.

It was agreed that each participating group was to have a representative on the Board. I was asked to be the first Chairman, but as my duties were already very heavy, I had to decline. I agreed, however, to become Vice-Chairman, and I presided at the early meetings till a Chairman was found in Thomas Beckett, a large storekeeper in Pretoria. The Government appointed Auditor-General Marais and Treasurer-General Boshoff as directors, and Dr Leyds as Government Syndic, with full power to attend meetings of the Board and to investigate the affairs of the Bank and Mint at any time. The concession demanded that the concern should be a State Bank.

The State Mint was under the control of the bank, and was established in a building annexed to it. As Paul Kruger insisted on having Dutch or German managers in control of the bank, the Deutsche Bank was approached. They sent out Herr Knappe, and Messrs Schroeder sent out Herr Militz. The former was a small, sturdy, dark man with a bald head and brilliant dark eyes. He had been German Consul in Samoa and, having fallen foul of Prince Bismarck, had been dismissed from the service. Herr Militz was a pale, fair man who suffered from an inferiority complex, and washed his hands like Uriah Heep whenever anyone spoke to him. He had been employed as a clerk in Schroeder's office in London. Both men had been selected because they could speak English.

As I wanted the institution to make a good start, I stipulated that all the banking business controlled by our firm should be transferred to the National Bank.

The banking experience of our two managers proved to be very limited, and it soon became evident that it would be detrimental to the bank's interests if their services were retained. There had been a tendency to grant loans to their friends on inadequate security, and matters soon became so serious that an official enquiry had to be instituted.

J W S Langerman, who afterwards became J B Robinson's right-hand man, and I were deputed as a committee to report and investigate. Our finding resulted in the two general managers being dismissed, and a deputation was then sent to President Kruger asking him to agree to the appointment of Mr Hugo, the general manager of the Pretoria Board of Executors, an old banking man of considerable South African experience.

Our deputation consisted of Auditor-General Marais, Treasurer-General Boshoff, Thomas Beckett, and myself. The President received us very curtly, and from the start gave us to understand that he wanted a Hollander appointed. He said that as Dr Leyds was then in Holland, he would instruct him to select a suitable manager.

I could clearly see that the time had come for plain speaking and a firm stand, so I told the President bluntly that through the appointment of inexperienced men the bank had narrowly escaped failure and that, so far as my firm was concerned, unless Mr Hugo were appointed I would resign from the board, and our support would be withdrawn.

'Moreover,' I added, 'a public statement will be made saying why we have done so.'

At this the President assumed a threatening attitude, declaring that I had insulted him. Marching out of the room, he banged the door of the Executive Chamber as an additional sign that he was annoyed. I took up my hat and told my colleagues that I was going back to the bank to hand in my resignation, whereupon Mr Boshoff asked me to wait a moment, pointing out that I was a very young man (I was thirty-one) to talk to the old President in that way, and that I should make allowances for him.

'Let me go and find the President,' he said, 'and see what can be done.'

After a little delay Boshoff returned with the President, who addressed himself directly to me.

'If you,' he said, 'will go to your bank and write me a letter setting forth all your reasons for the request you have made to me, I will see what I can do.'

The letter was sent, and Hugo was appointed as general manager, and Thompson Henderson, a sound man of good banking experience, was appointed as manager.

Curiously, our little difference made the President more friendly towards me. A few years later, when I told him that I was leaving South Africa, and would have to resign from the board of the bank, he said that he particularly wished me, as a personal favour, to become a member of the bank's London committee, because he wanted me to be his *waghond*.[1] I carried out his wish, and when I returned to South Africa in 1918 I rejoined the South African board of the bank, and ever since the amalgamation with Barclays I have been a member of that board. At the time of writing I believe that Dr Leyds and I are the sole survivors of the founding members of the first directorate.

* * *

Paul Kruger was very proud of his Mint, and it can well be imagined how he must have been thrilled with pleasure and pride to see his image

---

1. Watchdog.

stamped on a gold coin. However, the first effort of the designer caused some consternation in Pretoria, and the minted coins had to be withdrawn from circulation. The reason for this was that on one side of the coin, depicted in the coat of arms, was a wagon fitted with shafts instead of a pole.[1] This was a grave error, for shafts in a wagon were unheard of.

On the other side of the coin, however, a far greater outrage had been perpetrated, which caused the President to fly into a passion, for below his head was the name 'Oss,' and *os* in the Afrikaans language means 'ox.' It transpired later that the name of the designer, who lived in Holland, was Oss. These two mistakes were put right in the next design.

Soon after the bank had been established in Pretoria, banknotes were issued. When the first notes were printed the directors, at my suggestion, decided to present the first £10 note to President Kruger as a momento. It was a gorgeous affair, with his portrait printed upon it. When the day arrived on which he had been invited to attend the board meeting of the bank, the presentation was duly made with much ceremony. The general managers of the bank, Messrs Knapp and Militz, afterwards told the board that the note had been turned into gold on the next day, but this must have been an invention on their part, for the note is now in the possession of Mr Eloff, grandson of the President. To prove this, Mr Eloff allowed a photo of the note to be taken.

---

1. *Disselboom.*

FACSIMILE REPRODUCTION OF THE £10 NOTE
PRESENTED BY THE DIRECTORS OF THE NATIONAL
BANK TO PREIDENT KRUGER

Chapter 14

Boer Eccentricities

President Kruger set us a very difficult task when he asked us to assist in starting a cement factory in the Transvaal, one of the conditions being that we should employ a German manager and a German staff. None of these men were able to speak any language except German. All the plant had to come from Germany, and the factory was to be under the President's eye near Pretoria.

Lippert, Lewis & Marks and our firm undertook the task and found the capital. To protect our interests I became the Chairman of the company and took an active part in directing the concern.

From the start we had trouble. The Germans knew how to make a good cement with good material such as is obtainable in Germany, but were utterly at sea when it came to doing so with indifferent material in South Africa. According to their idea, the lime was of the wrong kind, and so was the shale; the gypsum was of inferior quality, and the natives ignorant and unreliable. It is true that they turned out cement, but of so variable a quality that even our own mine managers refused to use it. We had paving-blocks laid down on the sidewalks in Commissioner Street, Johannesburg, to show the people how good the cement was, but few took the risk of using it, preferring to buy the imported article, which had to bear a duty of 12s 6d a cask. At that time cement cost between £4 and £5 a cask.

Troubles of all kinds pursued the cement company. For fifteen long years it was a white elephant; it never paid a dividend, and the experiments, which were continually being made, ate up a good deal of the capital. One day the factory was destroyed by fire, and a new era set in. Mr Zeke Davidson, an experienced American cement manufacturer, took charge of an up-to-date English factory, and the company has been prosperous ever since under his able and efficient management.

* * *

In addition to the worries I had in handling the National Bank and the cement company with inexperienced German managers, I had to establish the Pretoria Waterworks without any rules or regulations to govern the working of the concern.

After the company had commenced work, it was found necessary to make rules and regulations governing the control of the supply of water. It must be remembered that Pretoria had no municipality in those days.

Accompanied by the manager of the company, I proceeded to the *Raadzaal* in order to explain to the members of the Executive what was wanted. President Kruger and his Council were asked to go, clause by clause, through the proposed regulations. When they came to the clause imposing penalties for wilfully damaging or putting out of gear meters and ball-cocks, the President sniffed, spat into the waste-paper basket, and said, 'What do you want such things for? Turn on the water and let the people use it. How can we agree? We do not know what a "ball-cock" is. What is the Dutch for "ball-cock"?'

In vain did the manager and I try to explain, but we made a hopeless mess of it in Dutch. Even Dr Leyds, who was present, could not translate the word. For a moment it looked as though they were going to shelve all the regulations, when it occurred to me to demonstrate the working of a ball-cock by producing the article so that the Executive could examine it.

The manager hurried off to the store and returned with a ball-cock, and after laborious explanations the regulations were all passed.

Some trouble was also experienced when we commenced the electric light installation of the town, because the President would not have any overhead wires, and insisted that we should lay underground cables.

The Waterworks concession empowered the company to impound all the water running in the existing stream. This was the only supply that the town had, and, from the year one, it had flowed in furrows through the streets, irrigating the cultivated plots belonging to the townspeople. The plot holders, whose rights had been ignored by the Government, were naturally up in arms against the granting of the concession, and were hostile to the company from its inception. When the cables for electric lighting were laid alongside and parallel to the furrows, the water percolated into them, and whole sections were continually being fused and having to be relaid.

It was no joke being Chairman of these service companies, for I was always having to go cap in hand to the Executive Council, asking for powers and pleading for the promulgation of regulations which would prevent the undue use of the company's light and water. I usually succeeded in persuading the Government to agree to give us what we wanted, but the fight with the townspeople did not cease till they succeeded in having the concessions cancelled.

Our efforts to please Paul Kruger by starting these industrial concerns not only cost my firm a lot of money but also made for us many enemies, for concessions were very unpopular.

* * *

Many stories were current at the time portraying the simplicity of the Boers, who, like all simple people, could at times be very suspicious. They, of course, could not realise how transparent they became when any deception was attempted. The following story will illustrate my meaning.

Oom Dantjie was a member of the *Volksraad* and a leading light among the old *takhaar* Boers. He had a good deal of influence, and his followers always consulted him if they had any doubt in regard to the way in which they should vote.

It happened that the *Volksraad* had under discussion a certain concession which was being applied for. There was considerable opposition to it, for during the first reading *Oom* Dantjie and all those who followed his lead had voted against the grant.

On the next day the matter came up for the second reading, when *Oom* Dantjie gravely rose in his place and informed *Mynheer Voorzitter*[1] that during the night he had heard a voice, and that the voice had told him that he had made a great mistake in voting against the granting of the concession.

'So convinced am I, *Mynheer Voorzitter*, that I did wrong, that I now intend to vote in favour of the grant.'

I was much amused and, after listening to the rest of the debate, I strolled out on to the square, where I met Edouard Lippert (the applicant for the concession). I told him that I thought it likely that he would obtain his concession, because *Oom* Dantjie, who had voted against it on the first reading of the Bill, had now changed his mind and had voted on the second reading in its favour. I also told him that *Oom* Dantjie had told the members that he had heard a voice in the night which had caused him to reverse his decision. On hearing this, Lippert smiled at me in his cynical way, and said, '*Oom* Dantjie spoke the truth. He certainly heard a voice in the night. It was my voice.'

The old Boers thought nothing of making as much out of the foreigner as they could. They thought that God had brought the *Uitlander*, as they called him, to the Transvaal so that the poor Boers might make something out of him.

One day I remember standing in Church Square in front of the old *Raad*, or Parliament House, talking to some of the first *Volksraad* members. One of them started teasing old *Oom* Toozen for having accepted an American spider[2] as a bribe for voting in favour of the granting of a concession to a certain party for the right to build the Selati Railway.

'*Die verdomde* spider,' said *Oom* Toozen. 'Shall I never hear the end of it? The rotten thing, it only lasted a month, and then it fell to pieces. No, that spider was no good. The only decent thing I got from those people was this,' said he, as he pulled a gold watch out of his pocket.

* * *

1. The Speaker.
2. A four-wheeled carriage.

I liked living in Pretoria and soon took an interest in the public life of the community, one of my first efforts being to assist in reforming the Pretoria Turf Club. I accepted the Vice-Chairmanship of the Pretoria Agricultural Society and the Pretoria Gymnasium, on the condition that General Nicolaas Smit should be Chairman of the one and General Piet Joubert Chairman of the other.

These two generals were great characters, and did much good work for their country. Smit was known as the hero of Majuba, and Joubert was the general who commanded the Boer forces when the war with England broke out in 1899.

Some time after the period of which I am writing, they both accompanied Paul Kruger to Europe to lay their grievances before Queen Victoria, and during their stay they spent a few days in Paris. There they were entertained and made a lot of by the President of the French Republic, who gave a banquet in their honour.

Kruger, who sat on the President's right, had on his other side a certain very distinguished lady, whose name it would be indiscreet to mention. She looked very handsome in her *décolleté* evening dress.

She found our Transvaal President extremely heavy on hand, and all her efforts to get a word out of him failed. On the other side of her sat General Smit. She wondered whether she would be able to get anything out of him. She therefore turned round to him and remarked in English, 'I am afraid, General, that I have not succeeded in making much headway with your President. Try as I will, I can't get a word out of him. I don't believe that he likes me, and I have been wondering if it is because I have a low dress on. He keeps looking down his nose as if he were shocked at me. Have your people any objection to evening dress for women? Have *you* any scruples about it?'

The poor lady got the shock of her life when Smit burst out laughing, and replied in excellent English, '*Allemagtig*, *I* don't mind, I wouldn't mind if you were naked.'

Chapter 15

The Dynamite Concession

The founding of the Transvaal Chamber of Mines on the Rand caused President Kruger some anxious moments, and I had considerable difficulty in persuading him that it was solely for the purpose of creating one voice and enabling him to deal with one body instead of with several different mine owners, who might each ask for different things. That was what always irritated and annoyed him.

The idea of forming a Chamber of Mines was first mooted by W Y Campbell, who represented Sir Donald Currie's group on the Rand. Campbell first discussed it with Lippert, who in turn came to see me, for, as I have already mentioned, he and my partner, Hermann Eckstein, were not on speaking terms. However, I discussed the matter with Eckstein, and he agreed, on the condition that he should be the first President and that Lippert should be excluded from the Executive. We then interviewed John X Merriman, who at that time represented J B Robinson and subsequently became Premier of the Cape Colony. After Merriman's approval had been obtained, he, Campbell, Lippert, and I met in Campbell's office and drew up the Chamber's constitution, which was finally adopted by the mines. That is how the Transvaal Chamber of Mines was founded.

Although we saw little of Lippert, I still remained on speaking terms with him till the year 1892, when I unfortunately overstepped the mark in speaking of him at a Chamber of Mines meeting.

I have already referred to the iniquitous dynamite concession which was being exploited by Lippert with the assistance of a group of German and Dutch financiers.

Feelings had run very high because the mines were paying for dynamite £750 000 a year more than the cost at which it could be imported. Although Lippert's concession gave him the sole right to manufacture explosives, the factory was a blind because all the material came from Germany and only the packing was done at the so-called factory, nothing being produced in the country. With the high profits earned, it was not a very difficult matter for Lippert to keep the majority of the *Volksraad* members friendly toward his monopoly. The Chamber of Mines was powerless to do anything but protest. I remember that on one occasion at a full meeting of its members I inadvisedly made a statement that men like Lippert should be put across the border and threatened that if they returned they would be hanged on the nearest tree. I admit that it was not parliamentary language, but, all the same, it fired the imagination of the mining community, who expected that my next move would be to carry out my threat. Lippert never spoke to me again.

* * *

The controversy on the subject of the dynamite monopoly had by that time received such wide publicity that Nobel's company sent some of their experts to the Rand to study the question on the spot. They informed us that the dynamite for which we were paying 150s per case could be delivered by them on the Transvaal border for 35s per case.

Upon receipt of this information, it was decided that I should see President Kruger and tell him what the Nobel people were prepared to do.

On this occasion I felt that I could not very well ask Nellmapius to come with me, because he was interested as one of the original concessionaires. However, he heard of my mission, and told me that he would like to come with me and help me to explain to the President the difficult position in which the mining industry was placed.

It was a lovely summer morning when Nellmapius and I arrived at the Presidency. *Oom* Paul, who was a very early riser, was seated on the *stoep* drinking his early morning cup of coffee in the company of some members of the First *Volksraad*.

As we drew near to the house, we could hear the President talking. He was telling one of his priceless stories, and we paused to listen.

'It was in the days of the old flintlock guns,' he was saying, 'and I had wounded an elephant, a cow with rather small tusks. She took to the bush and I set off after her, along the track which she made. As I ran I rapidly began to reload my rifle, and whilst in the act of ramming down the charge I saw the wounded beast in the gloom of the forest searching for my scent with her trunk in the air. Her ears were distended in order that she might catch the slightest sound.'

Here I caught Nellmapius's eye, and we could not help smiling as we looked at the old President, who was by that time entirely wrapped up in his story.

'The moment the elephant caught sight of me, she gave a scream of hate and charged straight at me. I promptly turned and ran back as fast as my legs could carry me along the track by which I had come, all the time ramming away at the charge in my rifle. Fifty paces ahead of me I saw a lion following the blood *spoor* of the wounded elephant. I instantly realised that although I might bluff the lion, a wounded elephant could certainly not be fooled. I therefore rushed straight for the lion. When he saw me and the elephant both charging in his direction, he turned and bolted. Then occurred the most exciting race in which I ever took part. The lion and I were running side by side. First he was in front; then I was in front. Behind us came the elephant, screaming and trumpeting———'

Nellmapius and I were spellbound, waiting for the climax of the story, when just at this exciting moment Dr Leyds appeared. Needless to say, the story was never finished.

The President at once got up and greeted Leyds, and we all walked into the house.

After we were seated I told the President that I had come to lay before him some facts in regard to the dynamite concession, and I asked him whether I might speak freely before the *Volksraad* members. He replied that he had no objection. I certainly waxed eloquent in describing the injustice suffered by the mining industry on account of the concession.

The President listened attentively to everything that I had to say, and then replied.

'Many years ago I was Commandant in the Rustenburg district, when an urgent appeal for help reached me from my friends in the Orange Free State. They were at war with the Basuto chief, Moshesh, and it looked as if they might be beaten unless they received assistance from us. I hastily got together a commando of three hundred men, and away we went to the relief of our friends. After enduring great hardship and severe fighting, we surrounded Moshesh in his mountain stronghold, and we could see that he was quite prepared to surrender. Just as we were about to reap the reward of our victory, which would have ended the long struggle between our people and the Basutos, the Imperial Government stepped in and took them under its protection. The Orange Free State government also received a message from the Governor of the Cape to say that hostilities against the Basutos must cease. At the same time an embargo was placed upon guns, powder and lead entering the Orange Free State or Transvaal from either the Cape or Natal. The Republican Governments therefore had to send agents to Delagoa Bay to buy powder and shot, but fever overtook them all, and they were never heard of again.

'There we were, surrounded by hostile natives, Cetewayo, M'bandine, Secocuni, Lobengula, Moshesh, and South-West Kaffirs. I shall never forget the serious position in which the Orange Free State and the Transvaal were placed, and now that I have the chance of making my country independent of England, you come here and raise objections.'

I explained to the old man that we should certainly not have protested if it had been the Government that held the monopoly to manufacture and sell dynamite, and if the huge profits found their way into the Treasury for the benefit of the country. But, I pointed out, it was too high a tax to pay to concessionaires, who did nothing for the people and imported the dynamite only to sell it to the mines at an exorbitant profit.

'Besides,' I said, 'we can buy dynamite elsewhere at thirty-five shillings per case.'

'*Jy lieg*!'[1] shouted the President.

To be told that I lied made me sit up, and I decided to try a big bluff. I drew the President's attention to the fact that there were witnesses present, and that I was a highly responsible person as Vice-President of the State Bank and a partner in the firm of H Eckstein. I told him that the offer I was about to make to him could therefore be considered as coming from a dependable source.

'Look here, President,' I said, 'I will sell to your Government one hundred thousand cases of dynamite, delivered on the Transvaal border, at thirty-five shillings per case. Will you accept my offer? Because if you will not, I must ask you to take back your words.'

I had him in a tight corner, and knew that he could do nothing without consulting Lippert. To give him time, therefore, I seized the opportunity of dramatically taking my departure.

Later on I was crossing the Church Square on the way to my office, when who should I see but Lippert and Leyds hurrying over towards the Presidency. I knew at once that the telephone had been at work and had conveyed an urgent summons.

A little later I was not surprised to see Dr Leyds walking into my office.

'Mr Taylor,' he said, 'I have just been told that you offered to sell the President one hundred thousand cases of dynamite at thirty-five shillings a case. Is that offer still open?'

'No, my dear Doctor,' I said, 'the President refused to buy, and I am not selling to the concessionaire. The dynamite is obtainable only if the mines get it under a much reduced customs duty.'

---

1. 'You lie!'

Chapter 16

Paul Kruger, Last President of Transvaal Republic

The reader will by this time have formed some opinions that will have given him a fairly accurate picture of Paul Kruger's primitive nature and of his struggle to cope with the march of civilisation which was encompassing him.

I have often been asked what I thought of the old President. I have always replied that it would never enter my head to say an unkind word about him, for he was a man who always treated me with great fairness, and during all the years in which I was in frequent communication with him, I had no cause to complain of his treatment.

He was a rugged old man whose life had been spent in the wilds. He was therefore uneducated and unread. He was a God-fearing man, brought up to deal with his fellow creatures strictly according to the words of the Bible and especially to the words of the Old Testament, which can be very hard. He was a leader by nature, and he never hesitated to accept all the responsibilities of a leader and even those of an autocrat.

From his youngest days, he had experienced what all the *trekboers* had considered to be harsh treatment at the hands of the British; therefore he disliked them. It was a dislike that was cultivated among all the *takhaar* Boers of the backveld. They claimed that the British had never done them a good turn, that they had been pin-pricked by the British Government from the day they had left the Cape in search of the Promised Land. Their traditions taught them that the British had ever harassed and pursued them, had fought them at Boomplaats, taken Natal from them, fought them again for the possession of the Transvaal, checked their expansion in the north and south-west, and refused to allow them to take Basutoland, Zululand, Swaziland, and other native territories, which they considered to be their lawful heritage.

With these convictions firmly implanted in their hearts, was it to be wondered that dislike should grow into hatred and blaze into bitter warfare?

* * *

It is impossible to say what might have happened had Kruger and his Government drawn their *geleerde*[1] men from the Cape instead of from Holland, but Kruger was certainly prejudiced against the Cape Dutch, because he had no faith in anything that came from the Cape on account of his distrust of Rhodes. He therefore preferred to employ people who had come out from Holland and those of his fellow burghers of the Transvaal who could boast of any education.

For a long time he was prejudiced against Louis Botha and Lucas Meyer,[2] in spite of the fact that they had been instrumental in causing a section of the adjoining Zulu territory to be incorporated with the Transvaal. He feared them as political opponents lest they should upset his policy of denying the franchise to any but his own people. He thoroughly distrusted the more advanced members of the *Volksraad* for the same reason.

He denied to the towns of Pretoria and Johannesburg the right to have municipalities. He had always lived on the veld, and it took him a very long time to realise that such public services as a pure water supply, sanitation and hospital needs were necessities of life. Therefore the

---

1. Educated.
2. Louis Botha in 1900 became Commander-in-Chief of the Boer army in the Anglo-Boer War and General Lucas Meyer also distinguished himself in the field.

tiresome regulations which governed them were beyond his comprehension.

Kruger governed his country with the assistance of an Executive Council consisting of the men who had fought in the field with him against the British. Moreover, in all his ideas and in every reactionary measure that he introduced, he was always backed by the people who came from Holland. They stood four-square behind him and gave him whole-hearted support.

The men who came from Holland were not, candidly speaking, popular with the British or with the cultured Dutch of South Africa. The prejudice sprang from all sorts of reasons, real, but mostly petty. The Hollanders, as they were called, did not 'mix,' and they rarely intermarried with South Africans. They kept themselves aloof. Unlike the South African Dutch, the Hollanders never joined in any sports.

Coming as they did from the country where the ancestors of most of the *Afrikander* people—as they were then called—sprang, they could not free their minds from the feeling that the Dutch-speaking people of South Africa were their cousins and still constituted a remote outpost of Holland on the route to the Dutch possessions in the East.

At the time of which I write the Hollanders had great power, for many of the permanent officials, most of the postal officials and magistrates, and nearly all the editors of the Dutch press in the Transvaal were Hollanders.

I cannot recall that there was ever even a whisper in condemnation of the commercial morality of these people, and undoubtedly many of them were highly educated businessmen.

I mention this because one used to hear, in conversation with *Uitlanders*, accusations against some of the leading Hollanders to the effect that they were willing to accept presents for services, which they were supposed to be able to render in obtaining favours for British applicants who wanted the support of members of the *Volksraad*.

I was, however, in a very good position during my residence in Pretoria from 1890 to 1893 to know all that was going on in Government circles, and I can honestly say that I never heard of any member of the Transvaal Government Executive accepting presents or bribes.

It is true that some members of the *Volksraad* used to accept small gifts from concession hunters, but the consideration involved did not in my time amount to a row of pins.

In later years, however, before the Anglo-Boer War, I know that there was much said and written on the subject of corruption among the Boer officials. I believe that the group of dynamite concessionaires, of whom Edouard Lippert was the head, did continually bribe some members of the *Volksraad* by offering them royalties amounting to sixpence or even more on every case of explosives sold, but I never heard this accusation levelled against any member of the Executive. Indeed, I had been in such close touch with so many of them that I could draw fairly accurate conclusions.

The obstacle with which I found it most difficult to cope was their narrow religious bigotry. For instance, I remember on one occasion a certain committee, which had been appointed in Johannesburg for the purpose of receiving and entertaining Sir Henry Loch, Governor of the Cape, Lady Loch, and their two daughters, had arranged a dance in their honour. This soon reached the ears of the President, who at once sent word to me asking me to call on him at the *Raadzaal*, where he was sitting with the Executive Council.

When I arrived the President pointed out to me that any entertainment given in the Governor's honour should have the approval of the Church, of which he, as President of the Republic, was the official head. He went on to say that he did not approve of dancing and, therefore, he could not give his sanction to the proposed ball. I tried to convince him that dancing was a harmless European custom, and that Lady Loch and her daughters would, I felt sure, like a dance better than any other form of entertainment.

The old gentleman looked at me with his beady eyes.

'You come to me daily asking me for favours for the Rand people,' he said in a pathetic tone. 'I am always doing what you ask me to do, and now that I ask you to do a little thing for me, you make excuses. What sort of friend are you?'

He then earnestly asked me to go over to Johannesburg and try to persuade the committee to substitute some other form of entertainment.

When I arrived in Johannesburg I went straight to St John Carr's[1] house, and there I found John Tudhope, Lionel Phillips, Jim Leonard, George Farrar, and many other members of the reception committee waiting to meet me. I informed them of my mission, but they only jeered at me and told me to tell Mr Kruger to go to Hades.

'What right has the President to dictate to us?' they said.

I reminded them that I had rendered very great services to the mining community by persuading the Government to withdraw proclamations hostile to the mines, by obtaining for them all sorts of favours, and by fighting those who were out to blackmail the mining industry. I also told them that unless they agreed to change their programme, all my influence on their behalf would disappear, and that I might as well leave Pretoria.

Wiser counsels eventually prevailed, and the committee asked me to make a suggestion.

'Will you,' I said, 'give up the idea of the dance, and substitute a concert with both sacred and secular music?'

I can see their faces now as they roared with laughter.

At last, however, they agreed, and the concert took place. As can well be imagined, it was a very tame affair, and I sat with Their Excellencies in the front row.

When I returned to Pretoria, I at once went to the *Raadzaal* to see the President, and he and General Nicolaas Smit met me at the back of the Chairman's dais. I told them of the success of my mission, and *Oom* Paul put his hand on my shoulder, thanking me with tears in his eyes. I had no idea that he had taken the matter so much to heart. He seemed deeply moved, and repeated what he had told me before, that, as head of the Church, he could not have sanctioned dancing, because the Governor's party were guests of the State.

* * *

I have mentioned that the President was a very early riser. He preferred to discuss any urgent matter between 5 and 7am. Meetings

---

1. St John Carr became the first mayor of Johannesburg in Lord Milner's regime after the Anglo-Boer War, and was knighted for his services.

took place on the veranda of the Presidency, and if he were in a good humour he would tell some of his exploits on commando or on hunting expeditions. Most of them, of course, were chestnuts.

One story which he often told, which certainly illustrated the personal bravery and stoicism of the man, is the one relating to the operation he performed on his own thumb, which had been terribly injured by the bursting of his rifle when he was on a hunting expedition. It caused him considerable pain, and gangrene had already commenced. He finally decided to remove the offending member. He therefore severed the injured piece of bone at the joint, using his own hunting-knife, whose last office had probably been to cut a plug of tobacco. The modern surgeon, with his knowledge of septic poisoning, tetanus, and gangrene, would shudder at the bare idea, but I doubt if the old stoic did. In telling this story of how he amputated his thumb, he used to hold his good thumb between his teeth, take out his knife, and demonstrate how he sawed it off.

One of his favourite stories was about a Boer named Erasmus who was travelling in his two-wheeled Cape cart on the Springbok Flats in the Northern Transvaal. One morning he inspanned his horses very early in order that he might shoot a buck for the pot. He and his Hottentot driver were straining their eyes in the hope of spotting a wildebeest or some other game, when suddenly a lion sprang out of the long grass and leaped on to the back of one of the horses, burying its teeth in the back of its neck and killing it instantly. Erasmus had been sitting on the seat of the cart holding his Martini rifle between his legs. This weapon was one of the kind that had a falling block-breech with a hammer and nipple. Percussion caps had to be used with these rifles.

As the dead horse fell to the ground with the lion on top of him, the cart went down with a jerk on that side, causing the hammer of Erasmus's rifle to hit the seat. This broke off the hammer, and both he and his Hottentot driver made a dive for the floor of the cart, there they lay struggling, each endeavouring to push the other between himself and the lion, which was growling as it licked the blood oozing from the dead horse's neck.

'The hammer of my rifle is broken,' whispered Erasmus to his driver, 'so I can't use it, but I will put some powder in the nipple and take aim.

When I say '*Toe*,'[1] you must strike a match and set fire to the powder in the nipple.'

Carefully aiming at the lion, Erasmus said '*Toe*,' but when the 'boy' scratched the match the lion looked up and growled. This happened several times, and so they gave up trying, and waited.

By this time the second horse was paralysed with fear, but he was soon put out of his misery by a bite in the neck from the lion. Imagine the relief of the two unfortunate occupants of the cart when they heard the driver of an approaching wagon crack his whip, and saw the lion slinking away into the long grass.

* * *

During my stay in Pretoria I frequently introduced distinguished visitors to the President. Among them were Sir John Willoughby, Dr Jameson, and many visitors from England such as the Duke of Montrose, Lord Crewe, then Lord Houghton, and others.

It will be remembered that Sir John Willoughby was Dr Jameson's right hand man in Mashonaland, and was in military command of the forces at the disposal of the Chartered Company. In 1891 Colonel Ferreira, who had been created a Companion of the Order of St Michael and St George at the time when the British were occupying the Transvaal, raised a burgher force at President Kruger's instigation, with the intention of invading Mashonaland. He had intended to cross the Limpopo River at Tuli Drift, and it was there that he found Sir John Willoughby, with a strong force, prepared to check his advance.

After this exploit Sir John Willoughby paid a visit to Pretoria, and I was able to arrange an interview for him with President Kruger, with the kind assistance of Dr Leyds. At five o' clock on the following morning we found ourselves in the President's *voorkamer*, and after the necessary introductions he asked me to tell him what business Sir John had come to see him about.

Sir John, in his quick, alert, soldierly way, wasted no time in coming to the point. He told the President that Colonel Ferreira had threatened to enter the Chartered Company's territory, and had been turned back.

---

1. 'Now.'

PRESIDENT AND MRS PAUL KRUGER

He then warned the President that if Colonel Ferreira persisted in his attempt there would surely be bloodshed, because the Chartered Company would be obliged to oppose any effort to force a passage of the drift.

'This,' said Sir John, 'would be considered as a declaration of war, not only against the Chartered Company, but also against Her Majesty's Government.'

Dr Leyds, who was present, translated most carefully what Sir John had said, whereupon *Oom* Paul carefully knocked the ashes out of his pipe, and said, '*Wel, as daar oorlog moet wees, laat daar oorlog wees*.'[1]

These words were not translated by Dr Leyds, and therefore were not understood by Sir John, who, having fired off his ultimatum, got up, said goodbye, and left the room. I followed him, and when we reached the street he asked me what the old man had said.

When I told him, he flared up and wanted to go back at once, but I refused to do so, and told him I thought it was much better to leave things the way they were.

After we had left the Presidency, the President told Dr Leyds to enquire of De Wet, the British Resident, under what authority Sir John Willoughby had threatened the Transvaal with war.

De Wet wired to Sir Henry Loch, the High Commissioner in Cape Town, and in due course an official disclaimer arrived.

Shortly after this episode, Dr Jameson arrived in Pretoria. He also came to me and asked me to make an appointment for him with President Kruger. This I had no difficulty in doing, and when the Doctor arrived at my house we walked over to the Presidency, where I made the necessary introductions.

Jameson was far more diplomatic than Sir John Willoughby had been. He discussed the President's health, complimented him on looking so well and vigorous, and chatted pleasantly on various subjects. Indeed, he hardly touched on Colonel Ferreira's expedition to Mashonaland, and only said it would be a thousand pities if the Colonel's hot-headed action embroiled the Transvaal in difficulties. *Oom* Paul grunted his approval of the sentiment and, after shaking hands, we took our departure.

When we were alone again, I asked Jameson what he thought of the old man. His answer was characteristic, 'Damn you fellows, you have

---

1. 'Well, if there must be war, let there be war.'

always led us to believe that old Kruger was tottering on the verge of the grave, whereas he will see us all under the sod.'

There is a curious sequel to this story. Just before Jameson left for Tuli he sent me the following note:

'28 May 1891

Dear Taylor,

Would you please send the following telegram.

"From Jameson

To Charter
Cape Town

Later. Have seen subsidised one who confirms the collapse of the trek from the head centre downwards. Have sent him with instructions for Meyer and Nicholson. Ends."'

I sent the telegram. Someone had evidently been squared, but it was no business of mine.

* * *

As I have already mentioned, President Kruger was a very religious man and held very strict views on the observance of the Sabbath.

In the early 'nineties I was chairman of the Robinson Gold Mining Company when the manager of the mine showed me a summons that he had received from the Government, calling upon him to desist from working the mine on Sundays.

I took the summons to Mr van der Merwe, the Gold Commissioner, and explained that, as I was chairman of the company, the summons should have been served upon me. With this he agreed, and gave me his promise to do nothing about issuing a summons on me till the next day, so as to give me time to visit Pretoria and talk the matter over with the President. The closing of mine batteries on Sundays involved a vital principle that could not be surrendered without a struggle.

I wired to Nellmapius to meet me, and together we called upon the President. Mrs Kruger happened to be there when we arrived, and she remained in the room listening to what we had to say.

After I had explained the object of my visit, the President rambled off into one of his stories that often contained a parable.

'When I was a young man,' he said, 'I took part in a trek to Angola in search of the land of milk and honey. My party suffered such terrible hardships in crossing the great desert that we were obliged to turn back. One Sunday we found ourselves on a fine grassy tableland, with lots of game about. For months we had not tasted fresh meat, and there, before our eyes, stood a herd of wildebeest close to the wagons.

'When my wife saw them she cried out to me, "Paul, be quick, take your gun and shoot one of those beasts! Even though it may be the Sabbath, it is the Lord's will that you should feed your people."

'With that she handed me my gun. I took the old flintlock, and aimed at a wildebeest. There was a flash in the pan, but the gun did not go off.

'"There," I said, "you see it is not the Lord's will."

'But just as I was in the act of handing the gun back to her, it went off, and in doing so killed the biggest and fattest beast in the herd.'

Here the story came to an abrupt end, whereupon Mrs Kruger looked hard at me and walked into the kitchen. Nellmapius and I promptly followed her and asked her what message the President had meant to convey to us by the story.

'You foolish people,' she replied. 'Can't you see? The President is head of the Church, and therefore he cannot officially sanction Sunday working.'

How dense we had been! We thanked the shrewd old lady profusely, and hurried away. The summons was never served.

Chapter 17

My Farewell to *Oom Paul*

In 1894, I decided to retire from business. Life had been a bit too strenuous even for a man of my age. When I was young, boys of my age amused themselves by playing cricket, football, and other games, while I was working in the mines. I had worked very hard and had made enough money to enable me to retire, see something of the world, and finally settle down on some nice farm. That was the height of my ambition. My wife was quite willing to lead a country life, and I am quite sure that our little boy, Gordon,[1] who was then nearly two years old, would have been glad to leave the town.

Having come to this decision, I thought that it was only fair to let President Kruger know my plans. I therefore called on him at his house, and told him that I was going to retire from business, and that my immediate intention was to take a holiday overseas.

I let him know that it was my wish to return to the Transvaal and take up farming, because I had long ago realised how necessary it was that someone with a little capital should set the people of the country an example of good husbandry and crop improvement. I told him that it would be a real pleasure to me to take up this good work.

---

1. Afterwards Captain Gordon Taylor, who lost a leg in the Great War.

I had for a long time had my eye on an estate called *Irene*, about twelve miles from Pretoria, which had belonged to my old friend Nellmapius, who had called it after his daughter.

Nellmapius had been the first man in the Transvaal to carry on farming at *Irene* on what were then considered to be up-to-date lines. He imported bloodstock and modern agricultural machinery, and produced everything on a large scale, thereby setting a very fine example. He was always willing to place his experience at the disposal of anyone who was interested.

After Nellmapius's death, which took place while I was still living in Pretoria, I approached the trustees of his estate with the intention of purchasing his farm, *Irene*. I offered the trustees 4 000 Rand Mines shares, which at the market price of the day was equal to £32 000, because the shares were then standing at £8. They refused my offer, and two years later I sold the same shares for £50 a share, realising £200 000.

While I was negotiating for the purchase of this farm, I paid a visit to President Kruger and told him that I was contemplating the purchase of *Irene*, and would like to settle down there, but I added that I had no fancy to become a landowner in the Transvaal unless I could obtain the full rights of a burgher. I told him frankly that unless I had his promise that within a reasonable period my son and I would become enfranchised, I could not think of settling down as a property owner.

I told him that if I bought the farm, I would be prepared to turn it into a demonstration farm for the purposes of showing what could be done by means of efficient agricultural methods.

The President listened very kindly to what I had to say, and expressed great sorrow that I had placed that condition upon my decision to settle in the Transvaal.

'I want you to settle down here,' he said, 'but I am faced with a very great problem when you ask for the franchise. If it were merely a matter of giving you and your son the franchise, there would be no difficulty in doing so, for I know that you wish my country well and could be trusted. But if I give you the franchise, I shall be expected to give it to all the people on the Rand, and that would mean a sacrifice of the independence of my country. That I would never risk.'

JB TAYLOR AND HIS SON, GORDON,
IN JOHANNESBURG, 1892

Against this I protested, and pointed out to the President that many men like myself wanted to settle down in the Transvaal, but that we could not do so unless we were enfranchised.

'Moreover,' I said, 'if we became burghers, we could help you to wield the rod of good government. The people of Johannesburg want to be your friends. They have repeatedly offered you the hand of friendship, but you have refused it. They only want to help you govern the country.'

These words of mine appeared to rouse the old man to a pitch of great excitement, and he stamped about the room, saying, 'No, no, you want to wrench the rod of government out of my hands, and hit me on the head with it. No, I will never consent.'

Then, shaking his fist towards the Cape, he shouted, 'I have read what the papers say, that Rhodes has stated in Cape Town that there will soon be a hundred thousand miners in Johannesburg, who will swamp the votes of my people. Rhodes wants my country. Let him fight for it. I shall be ready for him. I am making preparations for the fight.'

'President,' I said, 'if you and Rhodes are going to quarrel, and if it ends in a war, how can you possibly expect me to remain here and become a farmer? As soon as my place is built your burghers will come and destroy all my work. It is far better that I should leave the country.'

'Well,' he replied, 'if you must leave the country, I am very sorry, but I cannot do as you ask.'

I then told him that if I did go, I should have to resign my position as Vice-President of the National Bank and State Mint.

'No,' he said, 'if you must leave the country, you need not resign. I have already told you that I look on you as my *waghond*, and I wish you to remain a director and help us in London.'

This I agreed to do, and we then said goodbye.

* * *

That was the last I saw of the old man. I had a great admiration for him and his people. He had a very difficult task before him. He was a great patriot and a firm believer in the destiny of his race and in the guidance of his God. I can, of course, only speak from the experience I had gained from the time I entered the Transvaal to the time I left, that

DR JW LEYDS, STATE SECRETARY TO THE TRANSVAAL REPUBLIC, 1886

is between 1881 and 1894, but during those years I received the greatest kindness and abundant hospitality from the Boers wherever I went.

Critics of the old President must bear in mind that the advent of thousands of people to the Transvaal in search of fortunes presented many difficult problems against which he had to struggle. Much as he would have liked to have looked only to his own people for assistance and advice in the government of his country, he was shrewd enough to see that they lacked the needful experience. He distrusted the English and the Cape Dutch. His only course, therefore, was to engage the services of those Dutchmen who had come from Holland and settled in the Transvaal. Of these, Jorrison, Leyds, and others were certainly most capable men, and they did their best to help the President.

Dr Leyds was perhaps the ablest of Kruger's advisers. He was a highly cultured man, and had a charming and polished manner. He was a musician of some merit, and played the violin beautifully. It must be remembered that when he accepted the position of Secretary of State to the Transvaal Republic, it was understood by the Government that he should remain a paid correspondent of those financial houses in Holland that owned the Delagoa Bay-Pretoria Railway. He had no sympathy with British ambitions in South Africa, and it is regrettable that he made no effort to smooth over difficulties between the British Government and President Kruger. Had Louis Botha or Jan Smuts been at the head of affairs in the Transvaal in those days, before the ill-fated Jameson Raid, that ill-advised act might never have taken place, and probably there would have been no Anglo-Boer War to mar the close of Queen Victoria's reign.

I have had since my retirement many regrets that those left in control of our firm took part in political strife, for during the years when I lived in the country, I always made a point of keeping on friendly terms with the members of the Government of the Transvaal. I trusted them, and they trusted me. They knew that I had no inclination to intrigue against them, and that if I had any differences to discuss, I was always prepared to disclose them in a reasonable and friendly manner. The interests of our firm and of those people who supported us were commercial, and on behalf of those interests it would have been better to endeavour, by other means than by rebellion, to obtain justice for the mining industry. Had I remained in charge in Johannesburg, I should never have consented to the agreement made a year after I left with Rhodes or Jameson to bring in outside assistance to relieve our grievances.[1] The fiasco of the Jameson Raid and the subsequent evils that befell the country proved that I was right.

---

1. In December 1895, Dr Jameson invaded the Transvaal with five hundred armed men, anticipating a rising in Johannesburg. He was defeated by the Burgher forces, and was sent with his officers to London for trial.

Chapter 18

Percy Fitzpatrick

One of the judges of the Supreme Court in the Cape Colony, as it was then called, was Judge Fitzpatrick, an Irishman of ready wit and a fair knowledge of law. One of his sons, Percy, became, in his later years, famous, and was better known as Sir Percy Fitzpatrick. I do not propose to write his biography—I doubt not that it will be written some day. If, however, the reader were to ask for what Sir Percy was most famous, the answer in nine cases out of ten would be: 'For having written *Jock of the Bushveld*.' It is a delightful book, as everyone will admit.

What a raw boy Fitz was when I first met him!

I have already described my journey to the Lydenburg district and how I met Fitz. I little thought then that this freckled youth would become my lifelong friend, and, moreover, a great writer, eloquent public speaker, and one of the leaders in South African political history.

When gold was discovered on the Rand, Fitz decided to stay on in Barberton and take up journalism. In 1891, hearing that he was in low water, I sent him a telegram offering him the job of conducting Alfred Beit and Lord Randolph Churchill to Mashonaland, now part of Southern Rhodesia. I sent him enough money to come to Pretoria.

PERCY FITZPATRICK

Fitz was always only too willing to entertain Lord Randloph's party with stories of his adventures, as they sat round their campfires in the wilds of Mashonaland.

One night when they had all pestered Fitz to spin them a yarn, he had just finished telling his audience a hair-raising account of his escape from lions down Barberton way when a sergeant of the police called Billy Jones, who was one of the party, and had the reputation of being the local Baron Munchausen, suddenly called out, 'That's nothing to what once happened to me.'

Everyone round the fire pricked up his ears. Here was their local storyteller about to eclipse the stranger. They saw Billy quietly fill his pipe, pick up a live ash to light it, and this is what he said.

'Well, boys, I've had one or two adventures that I'll never forget to my dying day. I once started from my hut with a shotgun under my arm, and as I came out of the bush into a small open patch I spotted a sable antelope bull. Like a damn fool, I loosed off both barrels at him. Of course, I hadn't an earthly chance of killing him. He just gave me one wicked look and charged like a whirlwind. I made a dash for the nearest tree and leapt for the lowest branch. As the bull charged, his horn just grazed my posterior and, would you believe it, passed through a heavy leather belt I was wearing. He lifted me off that branch as if I had been a sparrow. I struggled and kicked all I knew, but he raced off with me through thorns and bushes.

'Suddenly he stopped. The bristles of his neck stood up on end. He pawed the ground with rage. From my terrible position, hanging on the horn, I could see another sable bull, bigger than my host, running towards us. They charged each other with a roar of fury. The attacker's horn just missed my belly and also passed through my belt, and dragged me on to his head. I managed to give the other bull a rousing kick on the snout, and off he went, leaving me on the horn of the newcomer, who was so mad at finding me on his head that he tore through the bush, scratching and bruising me against the thorn trees.

'All at once he halted. I felt a shiver running through the body of the great beast. At that moment I was horrified to see a lion charging straight for us. In one bound the lion leapt on to the bull's horns, which passed right through his body. In its agony and struggle to get free, the lion scratched with its paw at my waist and broke my belt. I felt myself released from my terrible position, and I fell to the ground. I then started crawling back to camp, which happily was close by. Bruised and scratched though I was, I suffered much more from the jeers that my pals hurled at me when I told them my story. I was so tired that I longed to get into bed, but I'd have died rather than have let them think me a liar. So I dragged myself along, with them following me, until we came to the scene of my adventure. "Look, and be damned to you," I cried. I had the satisfaction of seeing their eyes bulging from their sockets, for there lay the dead sable antelope bull. Beside him lay the dead lion, and hanging to his left hind leg was my waist-belt.'

I think that after this, before Fitz started telling stories of his adventures, he must have looked round first to see if there might not be another Sergeant Billy Jones about.

Fitz was a romancer of some standing, and was always ready to admit that only once had he had one of his stories eclipsed.

He could certainly hold an audience enthralled, and was always in great demand as a speaker at public meetings.

In their travels together, Beit had taken a great fancy to Fitz, and when they returned from Rhodesia Beit asked him to join the staff of our firm in Johannesburg.

When he arrived, I put him in charge of our Intelligence Department on a salary of £500 a year. One of his duties was to show overseas visitors over the mines, and I am sure that in the course of those tours round the mines he must have amused them with many a good story.

After I retired from the firm in 1894, Fitz remained as an employee under Lionel Phillips, who, with Frederick Eckstein, Hermann's brother, took over the management of 'The Corner House.' Fitz became a partner in the firm after the Jameson Raid.

Unfortunately, in my opinion, Fitz mingled business with politics, to which I had always been strenuously opposed.

All boys and girls who have read *Jock of the Bushveld* revere Fitz's memory, and it will therefore interest them to read how I was able to help him by telling him the story which I have already told, of how the wild dogs chased the poor little impala doe. Fitz worked this story into the 'Wild Dog' chapter of his book. It will therefore amuse those who know the book well to read the following letter, which I received from Fitz when the book was published. Not many authors are so scrupulous in acknowledging the source of their narratives.

'Bulawayo Club
Bulawayo
10 October 1907

My dear Jim

It was a shock indeed to hear that you were selling *Sherfield*; and now that you have sold it, I suppose you mean to put in most of the time in Scotland, as heretofore. And although it seems the more sensible plan to give up what you don't use much, it seems a wrench to part with the house you have made. However, it was not about this that I meant to write, but merely to apologise for a theft which you will detect in the "Wild Dog" chapter of *Jock*. I worked in some of the details of your experiences, or rather, took your incident with Teddy Blacklow in order to bring him in, and fitted on to it the essentials of another affair of a similar kind in which "Jock" was the chief performer, as narrated. I can satisfy my conscience because there is nothing which is to the credit of "Jock" which is not absolutely true. I wanted, for the sake of the old days, and a rare good turn, to bring old Teddy in. An incident similar to the impalas occurred here last year. George Mitchell came upon five lions hunting in line through old grass. He had no gun, so lay "doggo" till they passed; then ran back to camp for a gun; came back and couldn't find them; went on in search of a lost mule; heard a sudden hubbub and grunting, and ran forward, thinking they were on to the mule, but found the five lions grouped round a little duiker. In a second—after one glance—the lions scattered and vanished in a couple of bounds. The duiker scrambled up and ran straight to Mitchell's feet and stopped there. He, excited about the lions, ran forward with a shot, and, sad to say, a Kaffir knobkerried the poor little duiker. It had only a couple of small scratches on the inside of the two hind legs, no other marks at all. I have only heard from the Press cables of the publication of *Jock*. It seems to have been favourably reviewed by some papers, anyway. The hunting trip was a total failure. I shot two animals in sixteen days, exclusive of the brilliant beginning, three big ones in the first half-hour. I was among them. Abe and Hans were on the end of the "tape" all the time, and there had been no organisation or prospecting

Smuts and FitzPatrick

for game beforehand, so it was "change camp and move on" every day.

Rhodesia is a better country for mining and farming than people think. I have spent about five weeks here and have seen a lot of it. There is something in it. My love to you and Mrs Taylor, and the best of all good luck.

Ever yours
Fitz.'

I laughed when I received this letter. It was so like Fitz. He first candidly admits pirating my story, and then covers his indiscretion by capping it with another. However, all that is long ago forgiven, and until the dear fellow died we remained great friends.

Chapter 19

Cecil Rhodes

So much has been written about Cecil Rhodes that there can scarcely be any episode in his short life that remains unrecorded.

I remember a fancy-dress ball hosted by ten bachelors, of which Rhodes and I were two, before I finally left Kimberley for the Transvaal.

We decided to call it the *Decemvir Ball*, and the late Sir John Lange (then known to his intimate friends as 'Bubbles') undertook the office of honorary secretary.

Bubbles prepared a list of the guests to be invited, and we all met at the club to approve the names and settle other details.

Ladies, particularly young dancing ladies, were not plentiful in those early days on the diamond-fields. The elderly ones who were good dancers were therefore in great demand, and had a very good time.

Among the best of our elderly lady dancers, with whom Rhodes used to love to polka, were the two Misses C. They went to all the dances, and were much sought after because they danced amazingly well.

When Bubbles had read out the list of names of the guests whom he thought should be invited, Rhodes called out, 'Why have you left out the two Misses C?'

'Well,' said Bubbles, 'if you want to know, I didn't forget them, but I thought they were too old and too plain.'

Up jumped Rhodes, seized his hat, and made for the door, saying, 'If you don't ask the two Misses C, I won't have anything more to do with your damned dance!'

We rushed after him, assuring him that these ladies would be invited. The invitations were duly despatched, but Rhodes got more than he bargained for. No sooner had he finished a dance with one Miss C than he had to start off with the other. He wouldn't look at us because he didn't want to see us laughing at his perspiring efforts.

* * *

Although Cecil Rhodes bravely weathered the shock of the Jameson Raid, in consequence of which he had to abandon the office of Premier of the Cape Colony, and stand his trial before a British Parliamentary Committee, it shook even his wonderfully buoyant nature.

But there was still another fence for him to negotiate, for Kruger was demanding one million pounds by way of moral and intellectual damages, said to have been suffered by him in consequence of the Jameson Raid. Without any hesitation Rhodes had informed the British Government that whatever damages had ultimately to be paid would be liquidated by Beit and himself.

Negotiations dragged on for some time, and as Rhodes was anxious to have the matter settled once and for all, he called one morning upon Beit at his house in London to discuss a final settlement.

I happened to be staying with Beit in London at the time, and we were both sitting in his study when Rhodes burst into the room, and without saying a word of greeting, shot out his cuff with a pencil in his hand.

'Now then, Beit,' said he, 'what have we got to pay this damn fellow?' meaning the worthy President of the Transvaal.

However, no finality was reached, and the negotiations lingered on until the Anglo-Boer War, when the whole matter was shelved. Just before the war, Rhodes and Beit had actually offered to pay Kruger £100 000, but the old gentleman had refused to accept it.

CECIL RHODES

I have always felt that none of Rhodes's biographers have laid sufficient stress on the continuous friendship and support that Alfred Beit was ever ready to give to his old friend in times of need. None knew better than Rhodes that he could always rely upon Beit to do his share when the occasion arose.

* * *

Those who knew Rhodes well could not help knowing his faithful coloured servant, Tony, who never left him. The story goes that one day Tony asked his master what the word 'politics' meant. Rhodes did his best to explain, but failed to make much impression on Tony's mind.

When Jameson invaded the Transvaal, it will be remembered that Rhodes spent hours by himself in bitter solitude. Tony was grief-stricken at his master's distress. Longing to show his sympathy, Tony said, 'I am very sorry, Sir, but I suppose this is politics!'

* * *

One of Rhodes's greatest friends was Sir Charles Metcalfe. He was a partner in the engineering firm of Douglas Fox & Company, and was well known throughout the length and breadth of South Africa. He spent many years superintending the building of various railways, and he was responsible for the construction of the bridge over the Zambesi River just below the Victoria Falls.

When he was at Cambridge, Metcalfe was considered to be a fine athlete and tennis player. He was always in fine physical training, which stood him in good stead when he had to walk hundreds of miles, under very trying conditions, in the course of his work in connection with the survey of railways in Southern and Northern Rhodesia, where he underwent hardships which only men with robust constitutions survived.

Metcalfe had a keen sense of humour, and told excellent stories, which Rhodes never tired of hearing.

During his visits to *Groote Schuur*, Rhodes's beautiful house in the Cape Peninsula, Metcalfe used to amuse himself by working in the gardens whenever possible, gardening being one of his hobbies. Although when in London the papers described him as 'the glass of fashion and the mould of form,' he certainly could lay no claim to this

Rhodes gets news of the Raid

description when engrossed in his weeding and delving operations in the gardens. Dressed in baggy trousers and a shabby old coat, he would potter around, absolutely content.

On many occasions he was mistaken by the visitors for the gardener. He was often asked by them to act as guide, and was questioned about the shrubs and plants. He thoroughly enjoyed himself, and never once gave it away that he was only Rhodes's friend, and not his gardener.

There are very few of Metcalfe's contemporaries now alive, but if all his old friends were with us they would one and all speak of his very lovable character. He endeared himself to everybody, and I count him as one of my dearest of friends, who made life happier through having known him.

After Metcalfe's death I happened to be in Bulawayo, and was struck by the fact that there was no monument or street bearing his name. I pointed this out to the authorities, and was pleased to hear later that a square in the town had been named after him.

* * *

Alfred Beit was very fond of Rhodes, who on the occasion of one of his visits to London was complaining of not feeling well. Beit therefore made up his mind that Rhodes ought to see a doctor. He had a great opinion of Dr Schweniging, who had been Prince Bismarck's physician and enjoyed a great reputation in Germany. Indeed, all good Germans thought that he was the greatest doctor of the age.

Without telling Rhodes, Beit persuaded the doctor to come over to London, ostensibly to consult him about his own health, but actually in order to obtain the doctor's opinion of Rhodes's condition.

In due course the doctor arrived in London, and Beit asked him to dinner. Rhodes, of course, was there, and Metcalfe, Tommy Maquire,[1] Jameson and I completed the party.

During dinner Beit kept on asking Dr Schweniging if he might eat this and that, and what wines he might drink, and every time he asked the question the doctor simply shrugged his shoulders. Finally, when we had finished dinner, which, by the way, was a triumph of the chef's art, Beit turned again to the doctor and asked him whether it would do him any

---

1 Maquire, the well-known Rochfort Maquire, had obtained the concession from Lobengula for the Chartered Company.

harm if he capped his meal with a glass of Napoleon brandy. Again the doctor shrugged his shoulders, but he got up and walked over to the sideboard, where a few dishes of the food which we had just eaten were still left. Then he took a spoonful from each dish and mixed them all together in a bowl. Planking the filthy mess down in front of Beit he exclaimed, 'There, you will now be able to see for yourself—don't you think that this is sufficient answer? Why, it's a chemical impossibility.'

* * *

Just before Rhodes's departure for the Cape to attend the trial of Princess Radziwill, who stood accused of forging Rhodes's name to certain bills, Beit gave a farewell dinner party at his house.

The guests at the party were Cecil Rhodes, Frank Rhodes, his brother, Hawksley, who was Rhodes's solicitor, Mr and Mrs Tommy Maguire, and myself. I sat next to Rhodes at dinner. All through the meal he was complaining at having to return to the Cape in the hot weather.

'I know it will upset me,' he said, 'the heat of Egypt bowled me over, and to go back to the Cape now that the hot weather has set in is more than I can stand. Look at my pulse,' he said, showing me his wrist, 'do you know that it is a most unusual thing to see a pulse throb like that? It will be far worse in the heat of the Cape.'

Rhodes's fear caused so much anxiety that Beit immediately sent a cable to Cape Town addressed to Jack Stevens, the Chartered Company's agent, asking him to see Sir Henry De Villiers, the Chief Justice of the Cape, and ascertain from him if the case could possibly be postponed until the colder weather set in, because of Rhodes's condition.

To while away the time, Rhodes, Beit, Mrs Maguire and I played bridge. To my sorrow, I found that Rhodes and Beit , great as they were in world affairs, were dismal failures as bridge partners. About midnight Hawksley came in with the reply from the Cape saying that the Chief Justice did not think that it would be advisable to ask for a postponement of the case, because it might be thought that Rhodes was afraid to face the music.

When the sentence 'to face the music' was read out, Rhodes jumped up from his chair. 'Face the music,' he cried, 'of course I'll face the music. Damn the woman.'

This was the last time I saw Cecil Rhodes. He was nearing the end of his life, but he little knew that the end would come so soon.

*   *   *

I wonder whether people who live in the Cape Peninsula appreciate Rhodes's great gift of the mountainside from *Groote Schuur* to Constantia Nek, which he handed over to them when he died. It was a magnificent gesture of a man possessed of big, generous instincts, which had its birth when he was taking his morning rides over this lovely country at sunrise, often accompanied by Metcalfe and other intimate friends.

Rhodes was determined that the mountainside should remain free from habitations. He also saw the value of a road if continued from Newlands Avenue to the Nek. In fact, he anticipated the building of this road, later on completed by Sir Henry De Waal, the Administrator, by planting a double row of trees along the route, which he had had surveyed. The boundary of the land which he bought adjoined *Fernwood*, the property of his old partner, C D Rudd. Rhodes always cherished hopes that the *Fernwood* property would ultimately be embodied in his scheme, but this was not to be.

The avenue of trees planted by Rhodes began at *Kirstenbosch*. First came rubber trees, then camphor trees, then Spanish chestnuts, and finally oaks. It was Rhodes's intention eventually to have an avenue of trees bounding the road all the way from Newlands to *Constantia Nek*. He died before completing this work, but I sincerely hope that some day his dream will come true.

Sad to relate, the trees planted by Rhodes have been neglected, many have been destroyed by fire, some have been replaced, but in order to perpetuate Rhodes's idea of one long avenue, it is necessary that the Government should take the matter in hand.

Rhodes's wonderful gift has made it possible for South Africa to possess a National Botanical Garden on a large scale, and in a setting unrivalled anywhere in the world.

Since Rhodes's death, my old partner, Sir Lionel Phillips, and Lady Phillips, together with others, have made themselves largely responsible for the creation of this garden. It is a noble monument to all those, like

Sir James and Lady Rose-Innes, Mr and Mrs Bolus, and Dr Pearson, the first director, who one and all helped to create this national garden. They were aided by Dr Marloth, whose book on the flora of South Africa has become a classic. If it had not been for the financial and other assistance rendered to him by Sir Lionel and Lady Phillips, this great work could never have been completed. As a South African who has known them for fifty years, I must truly record my appreciation of what they have done.

Chapter 20

A Yachting Trip

Having finally resolved not to return to South Africa, I decided to take a house in England; and as I wanted to be near my old friend Frank Taylor, who lived at Bucknalls, I took a lease of a country house called *Serge Hill*, near King's Langley. There we spent some happy years, and my eldest daughter, Daphne, was born there. My wife and I both hunted two or three days a week in the season, and I managed to get a lot of shooting.

In 1895 I took a lease of *Gorhambury*, the property belonging to Lord Verulam. It was over 6 000 acres in extent, and had exceptionally good coverts for shooting, and good partridge driving. One year we shot five hundred brace of partridge in three days.

However, after a while my wife and I began to realise that living in other people's houses was not very satisfactory, and although it was very difficult to decide where to settle down, I finally bought *Sherfield Manor*, which was really a lovely place in Hampshire, near Basingstoke. There my two younger children, Lance and Iris, now Mrs Boyd-Rochfort, were born.

I had practically to rebuild the house, and employed an architect named Wade to do the work. It was an ideal place in which to live a country life, and it was very convenient for my weekly trips to London to attend a few board meetings of the two or three companies of which I was a director. I was always mindful of the promise I had given to President Kruger that I would look after the connections of the Transvaal National Bank, and this I did whenever I went to London.

On those occasions I always took the opportunity of visiting Alfred Beit at his house in Park Lane, and I spent much time with him.

The episode of the Jameson Raid and the trial were almost forgotton by the middle of 1896. Jameson was paying the penalty, and the Parliamentary Select Committee appointed to enquire into the implication of the Chartered Company in the Raid was due to begin its sittings in January 1897.

One day Alfred Beit told me that Jameson would be released from Holloway Gaol on account of his bad health. He had been suffering for some time—in fact he was described as a physical wreck—and the authorities had decided to release him from prison in order that he might undergo an operation.

Beit asked me what I could suggest as the best way to help Jameson to recuperate when he came out of gaol and had recovered from his operation. I advised a sea voyage, or rather a three-months' yachting cruise with a few of Jameson's intimate friends. I suggested the Mediterranean. Beit jumped at the idea, and asked me whether I would form one of the party, to which I readily consented.

Beit therefore chartered Sir Donald Currie's yacht, *Iolare*, and in due course we joined her at Marseilles. The party consisted of Alfred Beit, Jameson, Henry Robinow (a cousin of Beit's and a director of De Beers), Henri Bettleheim, and myself. Cecil Rhodes and Metcalfe joined the yacht at Naples on our return journey.

After boarding the yacht at Marseilles, we went to Monte Carlo and thence to Corsica, Bizerta, and Algiers, making trips into the interior of the country. From Algiers we went to Malta and Alexandria; here we left the yacht and went up the Nile as far as Assouan, visiting all the places of interest *en route*. I had bought with me plenty of guns and ammunition, so that we were able to get some excellent snipe- and duck-shooting in the Nile delta. Finally, we sailed for Jaffa, where we left the yacht, and went on a tour through Palestine.

We used to amuse ourselves at sea in fine weather by shooting with small-bore rifles, which I had brought with me, using little coloured rubber balloons, such as children delight to play with, as targets. We inflated them and let them fly from the stern of the yacht, and after some practice we rarely missed them. Every evening when the weather was unfavourable for expeditions we played bridge, one shilling points and five pounds on the rubber. Sometimes we played poker for fairly high stakes.

Beit hated to see anybody lose at cards, so he formed a syndicate, which he called the '*Iolare* Syndicate,' for which he bought some diamond shares on the market. The result was that when we got back to London, each of us received £2 000 as a share of the profit made by the Syndicate. As I had made £1 500 gambling on the voyage, the trip was very profitable to me, and enabled me to pay for a very fine collection of Persian carpets, which I had bought during the trip in the East.

By that time Jameson had sufficiently recovered to take part in the various expeditions which we made. In spite of his bad health, he was always good company. He was a man possessed of unlimited optimism, and when other people were depressed he always sought to dispel their forebodings.

When we got to Palestine, we left the yacht and went inland.

We made trips to the Jordan River, the Dead Sea, and the Desert to see the life led by the Bedouins. Beit had been advised to have an escort of armed men, as it was said that the Desert was not safe for travellers. An armed guard, therefore, consisting of a sheik and four of his sons, accompanied us. Picturesque brigands they were, but not to be feared, for they had only antiquated muzzle-loading guns.

From Jaffa we visited Cyprus, Palma, Crete, Rhode Island, etc, and then went on to Smyrna, the Dardanelles, Constantinople, and into the Black Sea. The weather was too bad to continue far into the Black Sea, so we turned back and went to Athens, spent some time visiting sights in Greece, and then visited a good many of the small islands, including Cephalonia, where the sea appears to run into the earth like a river, turning a water-wheel, which grinds the corn for the peasants on the island. Incidentally, the wheel is caked with barnacles, which no one seemed to take the trouble to knock off.

Through the Canal we went to the Adriatic Sea and along the Italian coast, ending up at Marseilles, where we left the yacht.

* * *

During the whole of our yachting trip none of us had ever spoken of the Jameson Raid. The subject was taboo. We likewise never mentioned Jameson's trial and imprisonment. We did everything to try and make him forget.

Apropos of the Jameson Raid, I only once spoke to Beit on the subject, and asked him why Jameson had gone off at half-cock. (I used that expression because undoubtedly Jameson started his raid into the Transvaal in a gambling mood.)

Beit replied to my question in the following words.

> 'Jameson told me that he started for the Transvaal on a sudden impulse, because he was convinced that the game was up and that President Kruger knew everything. He told me that in order to draw all the blame upon himself and save Rhodes, he had dashed into the Transvaal. He was gambling also on the hope that Sir Hercules Robinson, the British High Commissioner, would at once proceed to the Transvaal and prevent the outbreak of hostilities and the shedding of innocent blood. Jameson firmly believed that he could get into the Transvaal without fighting. He was kept fully informed of all that was going on in the Transvaal. He had read President Kruger's utterances as reported in the papers, especially when the President said that he was only waiting for the tortoise to show its head before he struck it. Jameson was aware also that Kruger knew all about the supposed Johannesburg rising, and that he was only waiting to prove Rhodes's participation in this attack upon the independence of his country. Kruger certainly had spies in the enemy's camp, who were suspected by the *Uitlanders*. Jameson told me that he could not be expected to wait and allow the blow to fall on Rhodes's head. He had to make a start, and timed himself to reach the Rand at the same time as the High Commissioner, who, he had been told, would immediately proceed to the Rand for the purpose of clearing up the mess.'

It must not be forgotton that Jameson had, acting as military chief of his force, Sir John Willoughby, who was prepared to take as great risks as himself. It is my opinion that Jameson was encouraged by Sir John Willoughby's impetuosity. Incidently, if my opinion is considered to be of account, I would like to say, in connection with the Jameson Raid, that it was Dr Rutherford-Harris who spread the report that Joseph Chamberlain was aware of Rhodes's and Jameson's intentions. I am quite sure that this was pure invention. In the same way it was never hinted for a moment that Lord Rosebury was in the know. It is so easy to say such things after the event, when the parties concerned are no longer with us to contradict them. At the time I was aware of everything that was going on.

I am convinced that Jameson had for a long time held the opinion that a row with Paul Kruger was inevitable. My reason for making this statement is owing to some remarks that Jameson made on the night of a lecture which he delivered some time after at the Royal Colonial Institute when the Prince of Wales, afterwards King Edward VII, was in the chair. We had all rolled up to hear him speak.

After the lecture was over Jameson, Beit, Rutherford-Harris, Sigismund Neumann and I went to Neumann's rooms, where we played poker. We played for very high stakes with a £1 ante. Everyone went 'blind,' and the 'blinds' were doubled. Jameson won £500, and I won £750. When the party broke up, Jameson and I drove home together in a hansom cab; and he dropped me *en route* at the Berkley Hotel, where I was staying. On the way he asked me what force I considered would be necessary in order to capture the Transvaal.

'Well,' I said, 'if you really want my opinion, I think you would require at least a hundred thousand mounted Colonial troops with horse artillery; or, as an alternative, five times that number of British troops.'

He laughed and came out with his favourite expression of extreme contempt, which I regret to say is unprintable. He was in a very happy mood that night, because in the last poker hand that we had played I had bluffed Rutherford-Harris out of three jacks with my pair of deuces. All the way home Jameson kept chuckling over this, because he disliked Harris.

SIR LEANDER STARR JAMESON

Chapter 21

Death of Alfred Beit

We were a very happy trio, Beit, Jameson and I, and although we tried to make a sportsman out of Beit, and always took him to Scotland with us in the shooting season, he never ventured to shoot or tramp over the moors with us. On one occasion he was very anxious to learn to ride a bicycle, but he never succeeded. Although he took his falls bravely, he never seemed to be able to learn to balance himself, and after breaking up all our bikes, he had to give it up.

He was quite content in just looking on while others enjoyed themselves. He bought a very nice place called *Tewin Water* near Welwyn in Hertfordshire, a sporting place with trout-fishing and fair shooting. His sole object in buying this house was in order that he might give pleasure to his friends. Occasionally he gave parties for the Ascot race meeting, when he would rent a house at Sunningdale; and on the occasions of the Naval Review at Portsmouth, he used to charter a ship for his friends.

His box at the opera was always placed at the disposal of his friends. He spent his money royally, and was a most intelligent giver to charities and philanthropic objects.

CECIL RHODES AND ALFRED BEIT

At the time when England and France were discussing their respective spheres of influence in the Sudan and Morocco, the German Kaiser was becoming very restless not only because of this *entente*, but also because Chamberlain was formulating a policy of tariff reform for the British Empire.

It was then that Dr Von Bode came over from Germany to London to pay Beit a visit. Dr Von Bode was considered to be a great connoisseur of pictures, old and new, and was head of the Kaiser's Art Museum in Berlin. As he was a great friend of Beit's, he used to advise him in his purchases of old masters, Italian furniture, etc.

Von Bode brought a message from his master the Kaiser to Beit. It was, in effect, that Beit, a German by birth, was doing so much for the British National Gallery and so little for the Museum in Berlin. The message went on to say that it would please the Kaiser very much if Beit would present some pictures to the Kaiser's Museum. Moreover, the Kaiser would like to see Beit on the occasion of his next visit to Berlin. As Von Bode was very anxious to obtain certain pictures for his museum, Beit bought them, and in deference to the Kaiser's wish presented them to the Berlin Museum.

A few months later, when he was on a visit to his mother in Hamburg, Beit received a message to say that the Kaiser would like to see him. In answer to this Royal invitation, Beit went to Berlin. The Kaiser received him very graciously and offered him the Order of the Red Eagle. Beit, who did not want this decoration, pointed out to the Kaiser that as he was a British subject, he would have to obtain permission to accept the Order. Thus he was able to refuse without giving offence.

The conversation between the Kaiser and Beit started on the subject of pictures, but very soon it turned to politics, for Beit and his host were far too astute to miss such a chance. Beit wanted to know what the Kaiser's policy was in regard to Morocco, and the Kaiser wanted to know whether Beit thought that Chamberlain could build his tariff-wall round the British Empire.

The Kaiser told Beit that he would not permit the French to acquire the same position in Morocco as they had in Tunisia and Algiers; and when Beit said that he thought that tariff reform would be the best thing for England, the Kaiser replied, 'If England builds tariff-walls round her

Empire, I shall have to decide whether England can be allowed to retain her colonies.'

* * *

Sometimes the American papers had articles about the South African gold- and diamond-fields, in which Beit was called the 'Diamond King,' and he used to say to me, 'Now, watch the next few mails from America, and you will see that I shall receive hundreds of offers of marriage from all sorts and descriptions of women, to say nothing of begging letters of all kinds.'

True enough, in a couple of weeks 26 Park Lane was snowed up with letters, black and white women offering themselves to the 'Diamond King' by the hundred! It was an amazing post!

* * *

The strenuous life which Beit was leading was bound in time to affect his health. For instance, in 1897, when the Select Committee on the Jameson Raid episode commenced its sittings in London, Alfred Beit had to submit to the cross-examination of Henry Labouchere, one of the Commissioners, who in his peculiarly offensive way subjected Beit to vile accusations, insinuating that he and his firm had been financially interested in the Raid, and that they had benefited by its failure. It is true that Labouchere was censured for his remarks by the Chairman of the Committee, but he could not be forced to eat his words.

Alfred Beit had at that time already resigned his seat on the Board of the Chartered Company, but continued to give Rhodes his active support in the development of Rhodesia.

In describing the effect upon Beit of the aspersions cast upon his good name, Seymour Fort, his devoted friend and biographer, uses the following words.

> 'Only his more intimate friends knew what a terrible ordeal it was to a sensitive man like Beit, who hated publicity, to give evidence on this occasion.'

It had been a terrible strain upon Beit, and this, together with the shock which he had suffered at the time of the Jameson Raid, and the flood of trouble of every sort and kind that followed in its wake, seriously affected his health.

In spite of this he continued his unabated interest in South African affairs, and was in close touch with his representatives in Johannesburg during the period covered by Lord Milner's duel with President Kruger, which terminated in the Anglo-Boer War.

When hostilities commenced, he lost no time in offering his assistance in raising volunteers in South Africa, and subscribed handsomely to their equipment. At the same time Cecil Rhodes's activities in Rhodesia called for Beit's constant attention and support.

Then came the death of Cecil Rhodes, who passed away at his cottage at Muizenburg in March 1902. Only his intimate friends realised what a great shock Rhodes's death was to Beit. It brought to a close a comradeship which had rested for so many years as one of the foundation stones of South African history.

From that day Alfred Beit occupied himself with all his might in the progress of Rhodesia, and in May 1903, the Board of the Chartered Company passed the following resolution.

> 'The Board unanimously resolves to invite Mr Beit to resume his seat on the Board, and in so doing to express to him the keen sense of obligation for the invaluable assistance which he has so loyally and unselfishly rendered to the Company since his resignation.'

* * *

In August 1903, Alfred Beit again visited Rhodesia and spent some time on the Rand. From there he went over to see the Premier Diamond Mine, which had just been discovered.

He left Johannesburg in the morning after a late night, and on his arrival at the mine he found that a very hearty meal had been prepared for him. It was also an extremely hot day. These circumstances and the exertion entailed in going over the property were the cause of a sudden illness, and he was brought back to Johannesburg suffering from a slight stroke. As usual, he had not spared himself in making a thorough investigation of the mine and learning all that he wanted to know. He was taken down to Cape Town by Dr Jameson and his friend, Abe Bailey, and from there he sailed for England under the care of Dr

SIR JULIUS WERHNER, BART

Jameson. By the time he had reached London, where I met him, he had made a wonderful recovery.

Beit told me that what had upset him was the fact that he walked all over the property of the Premier Mine on a very hot day after a heavy meal.

While some say that he was upset at the sight of what might turn out to be a large diamond mine outside the interests of the De Beers Company, I know that it did not cause him any anxiety or worry, because Mr Oates, one of the De Beers directors, of considerable mining experience, had declared the Premier Mine to be a patchy affair, and unlikely to prove to be of any importance.

According to Oates, the concentration of diamonds on a given area was due to the disintegration of soil containing diamonds, which had washed to one end. This was why the deposit was found in a concentrated form. Whilst we were having luncheon in Beit's house in Park Lane, I remember so well Jameson and Beit explaining this to me. They were both quite convinced that Oates was right, but I was the only one amongst them who had seen the De Beers, Colesberg Kop, Dutoitspan, and Bulfontein Mines from their inception, when only a few holes had been made on the surface. I had prospected no end of other pipes that had proved unpayable, including Taylor's Kop, Frank Smith's Kop, etc.

I warned Beit and Jameson not to be too hasty in coming to a conclusion about the future of the Premier Mine, because wherever diamonds had been found in payable quantities the mines had proved to be good. All poor prospects had remained poor. No diamond mine had become rich in depth when it was poor on the surface. I urged Beit to obtain an option to purchase an interest in the Premier Syndicate, and then do some prospecting work, but they would not listen to me.

It was the same when Rimer found diamonds at Kolman's Kop in South-West Africa. I urged Beit then to send a party to explore that country, for I felt sure that the small diamonds were wind-borne by the sand and that larger diamonds would be found if prospecting continued up-wind. I was laughed at.

*　　*　　*

FAMILY GROUP, HAMBURG, IN THE 1980s
ALFRED BEIT AND HIS MOTHER ARE SEATED IN THE CENTRE

There is no doubt that after Beit's rapid recovery he threw himself too vehemently into the work of his daily life, but it was impossible for him to take things quietly because his brain was always on the go. Gradually he wore himself out, and after a visit to his mother in Hamburg, he came back to his home at *Tewin Water* to die. His affection for his mother had been a guiding light all through his life, and she was the chief mourner at the grave of a great son of whom she was justly proud.

Alfred Beit was survived by his partner and friend, Sir Julius Wernher. They had worked all through their lives together in complete harmony, and few partners have supported each other so loyally and with such wonderful results. While Alfred Beit was a man of restless activity, Wernher was a man who loved a home life. He was a great reader, and those whom he admitted to his intimate friendship had a great respect for his sympathy and blameless life.

One who also lost a great friend in the death of Alfred Beit was Abe Bailey, who is still with us. From its inception Bailey had taken a great interest in the future of Rhodesia, and he has always been ready to lend a hand in any scheme in which the prosperity of that country depends.

Needless to say, after my long association and great friendship with Alfred Beit, his death was a great loss to me.

* * *

Under Beit's will, Rhodesia was not forgotten. During his lifetime he had given freely to charitable objects in that country—in fact he did even more in that way for Rhodesia than Cecil Rhodes. His will established the Beit Railway Trust, and it is due to his munificence that the Alfred Beit Bridge over the Limpopo River and also about forty-five bridges over smaller rivers have been built. In Northern Rhodesia, a large sum has been spent by the trustees in building a bridge over the Luangwa River.

Public libraries, museums, bursaries for educational purposes, annuities to indigent persons, grants to schools, playing-fields, maternity and child welfare work, to say nothing of grants to native missions and other social services—these have all benefited by receiving substantial assistance through Alfred Beit's generous foresight.

His will also contained a very large grant of money to universities in Johannesburg, Rhodesia, London (University College of Technology and Medical Science), Grahamstown, Kimberley, and gifts to hospitals in South Africa and England; nor did he forget his home town of Hamburg, since he left £20 000 to his mother for educational and charitable objects.

Chapter 22

Fishing and Shooting

Soon after I had settled in England, I rented Dalnaspidal grouse moors in Perthshire from the Duke of Atholl, and also the deer forests of Loch Luichart and Fannich.

Whenever it was possible to get hold of him, I always used to ask my old friend Mike Rimington to shoot. He became a general in the Great War, but I had known him intimately ever since he had served with the Inniskilling Dragoons in Pietermaritzburg, Natal. Young Allenby, afterwards General Allenby, was also in the same regiment at that time. Some years after the regiment left 'Maritzburg, where they were quartered for a long time after the Zulu War, Mike Rimington came out to South Africa again in 1899, and in the Anglo-Boer War he commanded a column of which Rimington's Scouts formed a part. He afterwards became Inspector-General of Cavalry in India, and, as I have said, held a high command during the Great War.

Mike and I always kept up a close friendship. On one of his visits to me in Scotland, he brought with him a pointer dog, about which we had heard great things. The night he arrived we talked a lot about this wonderful dog.

When we all started off for the moors the next morning, we could hardly keep our eyes off Mike's canine prodigy. Suddenly a hare got up in front of us. Off went Mike's dog after it, and no greyhound ever gave a better performance. We did not see the dog again for some time. At last our Scotch keeper, Gow, caught him and tied him up.

Gow was a good fellow, endowed with all the caution and canniness attributed to his race. When the day came for Rimington to leave us, Gow came up to bid him goodbye. 'Well, Gow,' he said, 'I'm sorry I have to leave, but before I go, tell me, honestly, what do you think of my dog?' Gow, not wishing to spoil the prospect of a good tip, said heartily, 'A verra speedy dog, Sir.'

* * *

In 1895 my old friend Frank Taylor and I took a lease of the Badanloch shooting from the Duke of Sutherland for twenty years. The sporting rights included a rod on the Helmsdale River, the right to kill fifty stags and all sorts of Highland game. The shooting extended over thirty thousand acres, upon which there were ten good lochs for trout-fishing, perhaps the best in Scotland, for a single rod could easily account for one hundred trout in a day's fishing, the average weight of which would be half a pound.

In a good year we killed as many as two thousand brace of grouse, one hundred and fifty snipe, and a large bag of grey-leg geese, duck, widgeon, ptarmigan, blackgame, and hares. It was a very sporting estate, and my wife and I spent many happy years there entertaining our friends and initiating our children to become keen sportsmen.

The salmon fishing on the Helmsdale in 1895-6 was so very good that Frank and I became very keen fishermen. In fact, I became such an ardent fisherman that I wanted something more than the spring fishing on the Helmsdale. Therefore I leased some fishing on other rivers in Scotland and in Norway in summer, and thus spent five months of the year salmon fishing.

Alas, a change came over the scene in 1897, when the salmon fishing on the Helmsdale started on the downgrade, due to over netting the river mouth and drag netting on the coast of Sutherland. This was owing to a lease granted by the Duke to Sellar Brothers. These dragnets extended from Golspie to Berriedale, and accounted for as many as ten thousand salmon and grilse in a season.

Frank and I quickly realised that our twenty-year lease of Badanloch, without the valuable spring fishing, would not suit us. We had either to sub-let or take prompt steps to do away with the nets on the coast and river. We also had to do something to replenish the stock of salmon.

I was deputed by the six angling tenants on the Helmsdale River to see what could be done, and in due course I was able to acquire the lease of the dragnets and to obtain a promise from the Duke of Sutherland not to let them again during the currency of the leases.

We bought the right to net the river mouth, and obtained permission to erect two large hatcheries, as well as the right to build two dams, one at Auchintoul and the other at Badanloch. I would like to say here that the erection of dams in order to raise the level of the water in the lochs, and so regulate the supply of water for angling purposes, had never been attempted before in Scotland, and it amuses me now to remember how overwhelming was the prejudice of the natives against anything of the kind. The dams were controlled by gates, and the water was fed to the Helmsdale River when it was low, so as to help the salmon to run up.

We turned out between two and three million salmon fingerlings into the upper waters of the Helmsdale and into the lochs that fed it. The dams enabled us to keep the river in good ply during the summer, and eventually the Helmsdale became a spring and summer fishing unrivalled for its size in Scotland.

I was rather proud of the part I had played in bringing all this about, for I had to overcome much opposition. If anyone is interested in obtaining fuller particulars of what was done on the Helmsdale, they can be obtained from Calderwood's work entitled *Salmon Lochs and Rivers of Scotland*. Mr Calderwood was Secretary to the Fishing Board of Scotland at the time. We collaborated and learnt a lot about the life history of the salmon.

I did not learn dry-fly fishing until I went to live in Hertfordshire. There we had Lord Knutsford (then Arthur Holland Hibbert), of Munden, near Watford, as a near neighbour. He was a very keen sportsman and a very fine fisherman. It was he who taught me to fish with a dry fly, a sport I took to wholeheartedly, and when I bought *Sherfield Manor*, with four miles of fishing on both banks, I set to work to make a first-class trout stream of it.

By resolutely netting out all the coarse fish and restocking with two-year-old trout, the fishing became extremely good, and trout of 4 and 5 lbs could be caught in numbers. In the 'Mayfly' season, there was practically no limit to the number of fish one could catch in a day.

* * *

I was very fortunate in having made friends with those who owned some of the best shooting in Scotland. This enabled me to take part, and—I say it with pride—a considerable part, in helping to compile some very big bags of game.

There have been days when I have shared in making a bag of five hundred brace of grouse in one day, and over two thousand brace in four days. There have been others when the bags were much smaller, but the parties were just as cheery and the memories are just as pleasant.

Having had a very hard time of it in my youth, denied all the sports and pleasures that other boys have during their school life, I was, when I settled down in England, really a boy let loose. Can it be wondered at that I enjoyed every moment of my life?

* * *

When I sold *Sherfield Manor*, I bought *Lyne Grove*, in Surrey, a much smaller place, with a park filled with beautiful old trees and a lake surrounded by rhododendrons.

The house was built in Charles II's time, and the grounds were originally part of old Windsor Forest. It was probably the residence of one of King Charles's many lady friends.

When I bought the house it needed modernising, so we set to work and made a really nice home of it. There my family grew up, and as it was near Eton, where the boys were at school, we were able to run over and see them occasionally. The place was also very handy if one wanted to run up to London, and I was always able to get a very good game of golf close by. Thus, when the war began, and I gave up shooting, hunting, and fishing, I was able to get a lot of fun out of a game of golf.

My eldest son, Gordon, was at Woolwich when the war broke out, and he went to France with the early Expeditionary Force in September

1914, serving as a subaltern in the Royal Artillery. He was twice wounded, lost a leg, recovered, and went back to France towards the close of the war in the Anti-Aircraft Service. He retired with the rank of captain after peace was declared, and came out to South Africa to take up fruit farming.

At the outbreak of the war the South African contingents began to arrive in England on active service, and I was appointed by the South African Government to serve on the committee that was formed by the various Dominions and Colonies to look after their men. Along with Jameson, Lord Kylsant, Otto Beit (Alfred Beit's brother) and others, I joined what was known as Lord Gladstone's committee. Its functions consisted mainly in looking after the men of the South African contingent. On those committees I was kept pretty busy, but was able to give some of my time to other movements such as the Victorian League, Peel House, etc, until hostilities ceased.

* * *

Jameson, Metcalfe and I saw a great deal of each other, for they both spent many weekends with us at our place in Surrey. They used to come to us for a fortnight every year in Scotland; and as each of us disliked the cold and wet weather in the winter, we used to try and get away for a few weeks to sunnier climes.

In 1915 we had a most interesting trip to India. When we reached Alexandria a battle was raging on the Canal, and our vessel was stopped. As soon as the Turks retired we received the 'all clear' and were allowed to go on. The attempt to take the Canal was very determined. We saw the bodies of the dead lying along the banks, and several aluminium boats full of dead Turks. We passed H M S *Hardinge* with her funnels pierced by 6-inch shells, and many marks of a recent engagement.

The Australians and other troops were entrenched on the banks of the Canal. A French battleship lay in the Bitter Lake, and we were told that her guns had done useful work against the attack.

On our arrival in India, the Government placed a special train service at our disposal, and we stayed at the Government Houses in most of the provinces, where we received the greatest kindness and hospitality from

THE CHILTERNS, WYNBERG

Lord and Lady Willingdon at Bombay, Sir James Meston at Lucknow, and Lord Carmichael at Calcutta.

At Benares and other places we were the guests of various Indian princes, who entertained us right royally.

* * *

In the winter of 1916-17, I went to South Africa for a few months with my daughter Daphne, who is now the wife of Captain Herberger, who gained great distinction at Verdun fighting for the French in the Great War.

Before we sailed for South Africa, my daughter, who had been working hard at the Slade School of Art, had won the coveted *Prix de Rome*. I believe she was the first student of South African parentage to win this prize. We returned to London in the spring in a troop ship, which was carrying a lot of New Zealanders on their way to the front.

The next winter I visited South Africa again with Mike Rimington, and it was then that I made up my mind to sell my house, *Lyne Grove*, and spend most of my winters at the Cape, where I intended to buy a little property.

After looking at various places, I took a fancy to the farm *Geelbeck*, in a beautiful and romantic part of the country near Saldanha Bay, where bird life and the prospects of sea-fishing offered great attractions to me.

I found, however, that this part of the world was too far from civilisation, and I felt that I could not condemn my family to the isolation that it would entail. Therefore, when they came out to join me in South Africa, I decided to settle at Wynberg, where I bought the property known as *The Chilterns* from my old friend Frank Spencer, who had established a vineyard for the exportation of grapes.

Epilogue

The cultivation and packing of grapes for the London market gradually became too strenuous for me, until at last I had to bid farewell to the home I had made on Wynberg Hill under the shadow of Table Mountain. I decided to settle much nearer to my beloved sea, where I could spend my days fishing from my motor-launch.

I am now in as good health as I suppose I have a right to expect at my age, and I realise that there are compensations in life now that I am obliged to lead a less active existence, for nothing can rob me of my memories. Among the happiest are those of the years when, with my family always near me, we together shared every joy that life had to offer.

Although I loved the twenty-five years of life spent overseas, yet I am glad that I came back to settle in the sunshine of the country where I was born.

South Africa reared me, and now I shall end my days not too far from the spot from which, as a small boy, I started on my journey to the north, into the new-found land that called me to help my father, mother, brothers and sisters to make a home, and possibly our fortunes.

Little did I dream, as I trudged along behind the wagons that carried us all to the land of adventure, that my lot would be cast in helping to supply the civilised world with diamonds and gold, two of the most precious of the world's gifts, around which romance and tragedy have been woven for countless ages; for since the dawn of civilisation men who have trafficked in gold have ruled the world, while women have sold their souls for diamonds.

Although my earliest days, as one of the pioneers of the diamond-fields, were full of interest, nevertheless I cherish most the memory of the later years, when I was privileged to lend a hand not only in promoting industries and a banking institution so essential to a community emerging from primitive conditions into civilisation, but, above all, in building up the greatest gold-mining industry that the world has ever known.

Today on the Rand I see fifty million tons of gold-bearing rock crushed every year, yielding all but about two-and-a-quarter per cent of their gold content, and I ask myself if the engineers and metallurgists, who have made this possible, will ever be rewarded with the world's praise and thanks that they deserve.

Few who read of this wonderful gold industry realise that millions of years ago the raw material was transported by water from its original source and deposited over hundreds of square miles in a part of the world which, before the year 1870, was hardly known to white men.

These vast deposits had been hidden away under a heavy over-burden for an incalculable number of years, until one day it dawned upon the pioneers that the upstanding outcrops of conglomerate rock that had been traversed so often, not only contained gold, but also were markers of the underlying beds which are now being mined nearly two miles below the surface.

Geologists are still wondering whence came this gold-bearing detritus, and if during its passage to its present site it left any of its riches *en route*.

In my day they used to wonder what secrets would be revealed during the next fifty years. Today they are still wondering, and I envy those who will be alive when the complete story is known.

Whether when that time comes the people of South Africa will have made the most of these marvellous riches for the benefit of the majority, no one can foretell.

I sometimes wonder if they realise that without the discovery of gold and diamonds they would have remained in bucolic obscurity, and that

JB TAYLOR, THE GRAND OLD MAN OF FALSE BAY

they have it in their power by sympathetic treatment to postpone the day when the Rand gold industry can no longer be carried on at a profit. For when that day arrives, they must, I fear, be prepared to relapse again to the status of a mediocre agricultural and pastoral community.

God grant that the common sense of those who rule the destiny of South Africa will endure, and that my grandchildren's children will enjoy the prosperity that my contemporaries have known.

Appendix

Fishing in Cape Waters

For many years the deep-sea fishing round the Cape Peninsula, and particularly in False Bay, has had great attractions for me. Fifty years ago I used to go out in a small fishing boat and fish off Sea Point and Camps Bay, and later I often went out in the fishing boats from Kalk Bay and fished round the Island when the wind was favourable, and nearer inshore when the wind did not permit of our going out to sea.

About fifteen years ago my wife made me a present of a boat, which she had built for me. I named it the *Lucky Jim*, and a few years ago I had a motorboat built in England. This boat was specially designed for fishing in False Bay—she was made of teak throughout, with cabin accommodation. She was equipped with twin screws, and was capable of doing about 12 knots. I named her *Daphne*, after my eldest daughter.

In these boats I have fished from Cape Point to the Strand in every kind of weather, and have had some remarkable sport.

I do not know of any bay that can offer such good fishing as can be had in False Bay. There must be, in the various seasons, upwards of one hundred varieties of edible fish to be caught in the Bay, and, provided they are properly cooked, they are the best eating fish in the world.

In bygone days, oysters were fairly plentiful, and may still be obtained at Strandfontein. Here may still be found a medium-sized sole whose flavour is superlatively good. Venus ears and *klipkous*, the largest variety of shellfish, used to be abundant, but they are no longer obtainable in these waters. The old Dutch and Malay cooks had a way for preparing these luscious crustacea that has long been forgotten, for you seldom get *klipkous* properly cooked nowadays, even if you are lucky enough to come across them. Perhaps the red steenbras is the heaviest edible fish caught in False Bay, although the black *kabeljaauw*, weighing up to 160 lbs, runs him pretty close in point of size. But the steenbras is a better eating fish. The white steenbras is seldom caught by line fishermen. They run up to a pretty good weight, so does the leer fish. The *geelbek*, or Cape salmon, come into the Bay in large shoals and may be caught at up to 30 to 35 lbs. *Kabeljaauw* are more numerous and larger, going as high as 50 to 60 lbs. In the summer and early winter, great shoals of snoek, mackerel and yellowtail come into the Bay, and are caught in vast quantities.

It is a common sight to see ten to fifteen thousand snoek brought into Kalk Bay harbour by the fishing fleet day after day, and the netsmen at Fish Hoek recently netted twenty thousand yellowtail in a couple of days. Lorries were employed to take these fish to the Cape Town market, but a good many had to be buried, because there was no sale for them.

Snoek are cured and exported in large quantities, so are yellowtail, but the organisation for handling the fishing industry needs perfecting. There is much waste, and the by-products are sadly neglected.

There are varieties of smaller fish such as harders, massbankers, and mackerel, which are also netted and cured. Sardines are plentiful, but are only used as bait—they are most delicious to eat when fresh out of the sea, but no one bothers about them excepting the seals, shoals of fish, porpoises, and the various kinds of sea fowl, often counted by the millions when chasing sardines.

Sharks of every possible variety are plentiful in the Bay. Some are dangerous to fishermen in small craft. Whilst my boat, the *Lucky Jim*, was fishing for snoek along with the fishing fleet off Cape Point, a shark tried to catch a snoek which one of the fishermen was hauling out of the water. The shark landed in the boat and knocked one of the men

PAINTING OF JB TAYLOR'S HOME IN ST JAMES

overboard. It was killed with some difficulty and brought to the pier in Kalk Bay harbour. It weighed about 700 lbs.

Once while I was fishing near Seal Island, in False Bay, a very large man-eating shark took from the hook a skate of between 60 to 70 lbs weight, and also at the same time a *kabeljaauw* weighing about 15 lbs, all in one gulp, leaving a piece of the skate's liver floating on the surface of the water. This seems incredible, but it is true. H M Turpin, the skipper of the *Daphne*, was hauling in the skate, and I was hauling in the *kabeljaauw*. We reckoned the shark to be at least 25 ft long.

When the sharks begin to trouble the line-fishermen, they invariably pull up the anchor and move off to another spot. Sometimes sharks will follow a boat, but not often. Seals, on the other hand, once they start taking fish off the line-fisherman's hooks, will follow the boat and continue taking fish. I have in mind fishing on one of the banks near the Island in False Bay. The anchor had hardly taken hold when one of the party hooked a *kabeljaauw*. This was promptly taken by a seal, which came to the surface with the fish in his mouth. It was a pretty large seal with an old scar on his back, therefore easily recognisable. We moved to another anchorage, but no sooner had we hooked another fish than the seal took it. Every time he took a fish. They were all *kabeljaauw*, varying from 7 to 10 lbs in weight. He would break the fish up in our presence, biting a piece off and throwing part of it in the air whilst he swallowed the chunk he had bitten off; then, catching the piece he had thrown up, he would bite off another chunk and repeat this operation until he had swallowed the lot.

We tried to get rid of him by sailing round some other boats at anchor, but it was of no use, and although we moved two miles away he started taking our fish as soon as we anchored. In all he took twelve *kabeljaauw*, the largest being about 20 lbs.

Line- and net-fishermen all over the world have complained to their governments about the depredations of seals, but numerous reports made by experts have been handed to these governments, affirming that seals do *not* live on fish and should not be destroyed, because, they say, many hundreds of seals have been killed and their stomachs examined, with no signs of fish in them.

From long experience not only in South African waters, but also from twenty-five years' experience on the east coast of Sutherland in

Scotland, I can positively affirm that seals do an enormous amount of damage, and should be kept under control.

Fishing on the Helmsdale River in Scotland over a long period of years, I found, in the spring of the year, that every seventh fish had seal marks on it.

The South African Government used to destroy two thousand seals a year and sell the pelts, but when the pelts ceased to yield any profit, the Government gave up killing seals. The result has been that for the last fifteen years the seals along the South African coast have become so numerous that they are a menace to the fishing industry.